Just Believe

THE TEN PRINCIPLES OF THE MESSAGE

Just Believe

THE TEN PRINCIPLES OF THE MESSAGE

Tracy J. Trost

with

Jim Stovall

DESTINY IMAGE® PUBLISHERS, INC.
P.O. Box 310, Shippensburg, PA 17257-0310

For a U.S. bookstore nearest you, call 1-800-722-6774.
For more information on foreign distributors, call
717-532-3040.

Reach us on the Internet:
www.destinyimage.com
www.TrostMovingPictures.com
www.narrativetv.com

ISBN 13 TP: 978-0-7684-3788-1
ISBN 10: 0-7684-3788-1
ISBN 13 E-book: 978-0-7684-8993-4

For Worldwide Distribution, Printed in the U.S.A.

1 2 3 4 5 6 7 8 9 10 11 / 13 12 11

Dedication

This book is dedicated to my beautiful wife Denise and my children, Greg, Wesley, Austin, Haiden, and Joscelyn.

It is your belief in me that allows me to *Just Believe*; anything is possible.

Acknowledgments

There are some moments in life that you experience where you walk away knowing you will never be the same. That is how I felt after my first meeting with Jim Stovall. Jim is one of those people who can present you with a question, and when you walk away you realize you need to make some changes in your life. Thank you, Jim, for your willingness to join forces with me to impact the world around us.

I would also like to thank the staff at NTN and, in particular, Dorothy Thompson for her Herculean effort to bring this book to press.

I would like to acknowledge Don Green at the Napoleon Hill Foundation for allowing us to use the wisdom and insight of Napoleon Hill. Steve Forbes, Harland Stonecipher, Paula Marshall, and the other people who have populated this fictional tale.

I would also like to acknowledge Tom and Marilyn Jestus—friends, counselors, and mentors. Your sowing in my life is reaping huge returns.

A special thank you to my staff at Trost Moving Pictures and Trost Consulting. Your hard work and dedication is allowing these dreams to come true. A special acknowledgment to Joseph Jestus, Carol Cummings and Evan Uyetake

Table of Contents

Foreword

I have written 15 previous books, and all of them are very special to me in one way or another. Each book seems to take on a life of its own as it is being written and when it is released to the world. At this writing, I have had five of my books either made into a movie or currently in production. It is a wonderful transition when the characters you have created in your mind pour onto the page and then are projected onto a movie screen.

This book you hold in your hands is a companion to the novel and movie entitled *The Lamp*. *The Lamp* is a very special story to me because of how it came to life. In 1994, I had the privilege of being asked to do a series of arena speeches with the legendary author Og Mandino. If you haven't read Og Mandino's books, you are in for a treat. It was late in his life, and the promoter had told me that while I was on the speaking tour with Og Mandino, I would have to be ready to carry the program and do an hour-and-a-half or two hours of material if Og wasn't feeling well, but I might only do 20 or 30 minutes if he was having a good day. This didn't bother me as I was just excited to work with one of the greatest writers and creative forces of his generation.

About eight weeks before our first arena event, the promoter called me to let me know that we had a "slight problem" with the tour. He went on to explain that the previous night, Og Mandino had passed away. I told the promoter that if this was a "slight problem", I didn't want to be around if we had a major issue. He asked me what I wanted to do, and I gave him the only reasonable response, which was to simply cancel the tour.

That promoter, who has become a dear friend, said, "Before I cancel the tour, think about what you might do if you had an arena full of people and three hours to fill."

After thinking about it, I came up with an idea for a motivational/inspirational live variety show entitled *Discover Your Destiny*. The program included live music, audience participation, kids and celebrities on the big screen, my speech, and a one-act play I wrote entitled *The Lamp*. I actually played the part of Stanley myself, and my friend and talented colleague, Kelly Morrison, played Lisa. Since my acting from that time 'til now has been limited to brief cameos in all of the movies based on my books, it has become obvious to me that my talent lies in writing stories and dialogue for real actors.

Several years later, I expanded the one-act play into a book, and then in 2010 after completing our first movie together entitled *A Christmas Snow* with my friend and partner Tracy Trost, I shared *The Lamp* novel with him and was delighted that he saw the same potential for a movie that I had seen.

Foreword

In these pages, you will relive Stanley and Lisa's loss and their struggle to believe. You will learn about the power that Stanley and Lisa discovered through an old oil lamp. You will come to the same realization that they did as you understand that the real power is and has always been inside of you if you are willing to just believe.

Through millions of books in print, including the one you hold in your hands, I have the privilege of sharing hope and possibilities with people around the world. As I have done with each of those people, I would like to extend an offer to you. From this point forward, any time your troubles seem too great or you doubt in your own power to just believe, please email me (Jim@JimStovall. com), and I will correspond with you personally as we engage your power and potential as you explore the ability to *Just Believe.*

Jim Stovall
May 2011

Preface

Dear Reader,

The story you are about to read is one that is very near and dear to my heart. It is not so much the people or the events in the story that mean so much to me as it is The Message that exudes from it. I was fortunate enough to meet Stanley and Lisa Walters when my friend and business partner Jim Stovall introduced us. Mind you, this was not your typical introduction. There was no formal meeting at a nice restaurant over a dinner or gathering of friends in a home. No this was an unusual meeting. You see, Stan and Lisa lived inside of a book. This book was written over 15 years before I was introduced to them

We had just finished filming our second feature film at Trost Moving Pictures, *A Christmas Snow*. Jim was telling me about Stanley and Lisa Walters and the lesson they had learned in their life through an encounter with a mysterious messenger named Charles. Stanley and Lisa had gone through some hard times, and they were pretty much at the end of their ropes. Then one day they were given a very special gift that brought them more than they could have ever expected. This gift was not like any other you would expect. It was not something that you could put your hands on, as it is more of a thought process than a tangible item.

After I read the book, I had to meet Stan and Lisa. I had to know more about their experience with Charles and what they had learned. I needed to know more about how they applied the principles that Charles had given them.

A meeting was arranged at a nice restaurant on the shores of the Arkansas River just south of Tulsa on a warm spring evening. Stanley and Lisa arrived on time with a sense of curiosity on their faces. They didn't know what the meeting was about. They only knew that I had heard about their story and wanted to know more. As we ate dinner, the two of them began to recount the events of their lives of almost 20 years ago. How they were both at their wits' end and how they both had found a new way of thinking which eventually allowed them to gain their hearts' desires.

This was the first of many meetings that continued for a few years. There was one meeting that I remember in particular, after our friendship was to a point where they trusted me with more personal information. Stanley reached into his computer bag and took out a manuscript for a book. I could see clearly on the cover page *JUST BELIEVE*. I asked what it was, and he said it was their story—what they had gone through with the loss of their son and how meeting Charles and being able to "Just Believe" had changed their lives.

Preface

I took it home that night and read it through in one sitting. I was captivated by their story and how two simple words had changed their lives. I knew at that moment, this story had to be told. Being a filmmaker, it only made sense to turn it into a movie. So in the fall of 2010, my partner Jim Stovall and I did just that. You may know the movie as *The Lamp* staring Jason London, Meredith Salenger, L. Scott Caldwell (Rose from *Lost*), Muse Watson (Mike Franks from *NCIS*), and Academy Award Winner Louis Gossett Jr.

Turning someone's life story into a movie is a challenge because you only have 90 minutes to fit in years of experiences. You only get a small taste of all that happened and what they experienced during those events.

This book is Stan's story and what he experienced when The Messenger Charles visited him. I hope you learn as much from this story as I did.

To your success!
Tracy J. Trost

Chapter One

Lisa

"A bell is not a bell until it is rung. A song is not a song until you sing it. Love in your heart is not put there to stay. Love is not love until you give it away."

Oscar Hammerstein II

The first time I saw her was one of those moments I will never forget.

Much like some of the other big events in life, I remember the moment vividly as if I could teleport myself there at any moment. There are few moments like this in life. For example, when I heard that President Reagan had been shot. I can go back to that moment in my head at just the mention of his name. I was 12 years old driving down an old country road with my mother. She had just picked me up from a friend's house and we were headed to the local Tom Thumb to pick up some groceries before heading home. We were listening to the radio and the announcer came on after a song ended and said, "Breaking News! President Reagan has been shot."

Just Believe

That moment has forever been fused in my brain, and I can replay it at any moment.

The first time I saw Lisa Schmidt, that was her name before we were married, is one of those very same moments that are etched in my brain. I was a senior at Oklahoma State in Stillwater, Oklahoma. I was going to college on a baseball scholarship from my hometown of Tulsa. I loved playing baseball. It was all I ever wanted to do. From the time I was old enough to hold a glove, I would be playing with my father or friends. I went through all of the traditional training with Little League all the way through high school. They told me I was a natural. I could play any position. I could even pitch. Of all the different positions on a team, shortstop was my favorite. I loved the pace of it. There was always action, and I loved the feeling of throwing a guy out at first base. There was nothing like it. There still isn't anything that gets my blood flowing like baseball.

In my senior year of high school, I was playing at the top of my game. I had broken several high school records. For batting, I had an average of .460. My coach had arranged for a scout from Oklahoma State University (OSU) to come to see me play. After the game, the scout came up to me and offered me a full ride. My dad was so proud.

My father had played ball as a kid, but he wasn't able to keep playing because his family was not able to send him to college. He was drafted right out of high school and went to war representing the USA in the Vietnam Conflict. He served two terms and then came back home.

Lisa

He married his high school sweetheart, and 11 months later I came along. He took a job to support his family and any dreams of playing ball were traded for providing food and a home for his family. My birth was difficult on my mother, and the doctors told her she wouldn't be able to have any more children.

My father was OK with that. He had his boy, and his boy was going to be a ball player—and I was. I loved the game, and I loved spending time with my father.

This brings me back to the first time I saw Lisa. I was playing in a ball game with OSU. It was early in the season. I love the spring. It was just starting to get warm outside, the trees were budding, and love was in the air. As I said, this is one of those times that I will never forget, for two reasons really. First, when I saw Lisa, I couldn't take my eyes off of her. Secondly, because I was staring at her, I completely lost track of the game. The batter hit a nice line drive right at me, and the ball hit me square in the chest. I didn't know what hit me.

The ball knocked the wind out of me and left a welt the size of a grapefruit on my chest for a month. I went down hard but snapped to it, got up, and grabbed the ball. I could hardly breathe, but I threw the ball to the second baseman and called a time out. The runner made it to first base safely. My coach just about had a coronary. I could hear him screaming all kinds of colorful metaphors from the dugout. All I could do was apologize and go sit on the bench until I could get my wind back. I was a little embarrassed though. Thankfully, I was the only one that knew that the reason I missed the ball was because I was staring at a girl. I could hardly look at her after that. I will never forget the look of concern on her face. *"I think she already likes me,"* I thought to myself. I knew at that moment, as I watched her in the stands, that she was going to be my wife.

Lisa was our first baseman Steven Yankel's sister. She was in town with her family to visit and to catch the game. They had planned to head back home right after the game. Steven had been trying to set me up with her for quite some time. He would invite me to come home for breaks to meet her. I just declined. I wanted to go home to be with my family anyhow. Besides, being "set up" on a blind date had such a negative vibe to it. You know what it's like. If she is so great, why does she need to be set up? Besides with baseball and school, what time did I have for girls? I was a ball player and I was going to go pro. I had plans. A girl was just going to make things difficult. But then I saw her walking down the stairs in the bleachers. He didn't tell me how beautiful she was. She entranced me. I couldn't take my eyes off of her. Why didn't he tell me she was so beautiful?

At the end of the game, I was all over him about her.

"Dude, why didn't you tell me she was so beautiful?!"

He looked at me with a bit of disbelief. "What! I have been trying to get you to meet her for almost four years now," he said as he punched me in the arm.

"Well, I want to meet her now," I said.

He just looked at me and smirked and then he said, "Well, I don't know if I want to introduce you now, ya big jerk."

Lisa

Just then Lisa peeked her head around the corner of the dugout and said, "Hi Stevie."

I had to laugh. I had never heard anyone call him Stevie before. He knew what I was thinking. He gave me a dirty look as he walked over to her and gave her a hug.

"Come on, let's go," he said to her.

As he said that, he looked at me with a huge grin, knowing that I wanted to meet her. She looked at me and smiled. I will never forget that smile. Then they turned to walk away.

"Wait!" I yelled.

It just came out. I didn't mean to yell *Wait*, but now they were both looking at me. Lisa was looking at me with anticipation as to what I was going to say next. Steven was looking at me with an *I got you sucka* expression on his face.

"Are you guys going to go to The Grind after this?" I asked.

Lisa looked to Steven, wondering if they were going to go. Steven, being the dog that he is, said "Oh no, I'm kinda tired, and Lisa really doesn't like coffee. So I think we will just head out."

Lisa jumped in, "I am sure they have other things than coffee, and it would be rude just to take off without saying good-bye to your friend."

She smiled at both of us, and at that moment both Steven and I knew she wanted to meet me.

Steven laughed out loud for a moment and then said, "OK. Let's go. But I gotta warn you about this guy. He is no fun. Everything is baseball with this one."

Just Believe

That was the beginning for us. The future was bright. Lisa was attending The University of Oklahoma (OU) in Norman, Oklahoma, which happened to be a rival school. She was going to school to be a physical therapist. She loves the human body and the study of it. She wanted to work with injured people who needed to be "rebuilt," as she would put it. After that meeting at the game, we were together as much as possible.

Norman is about 65 miles from Stillwater. Depending on my ball schedule, she would come visit me on the weekends or I would head down there. On the days that we couldn't be together, we talked on the phone. This was the routine for the following year.

The next spring, I graduated and was picked up by the Texas Rangers baseball team. This was a dream come true. I was going to play for a Major League team and be able to live in Tulsa. Most teams have Minor League or Double-A teams that they put their new recruits in to play until they feel they are seasoned enough to play pro ball.

The Rangers just happened to own the Tulsa Drillers who had a stadium about 5 miles from where I grew up. I remember going to countless games there with my dad. Since Oklahoma doesn't have a Major League Baseball team, the Drillers are the biggest thing there.

This added about one hundred more miles between Lisa and me. With my baseball schedule, I was usually out of town playing a game on the weekends. This made it difficult for us to be together. So we did what most young people who are in love and can't stand to be apart do. We decided to get married.

Lisa could transfer to the Tulsa campus and finish her school out there. I was getting paid to play baseball. Not much mind you, but I was getting paid. My father said I was being too impulsive. He said we should wait until Lisa graduated, and until I got more established with the team. My mother just cried and said it was beautiful. Both my parents really loved Lisa, so once the initial shock wore off, they were excited to have her join the family.

Neither of us were really churchgoers at the time. Since Lisa had grown up going to the Lutheran church, we decided to get married there. I can still see her walking down the aisle to me, dressed all in white with a huge smile on her face. Of course I cried. Lisa's brother Steven was my best man and made fun of me during the best man's speech at the reception.

The next few years went by quickly. Lisa graduated from school with her degree in physical therapy and personal training. She promptly got a job at an exclusive gym training the members. She was happy and loved what she did. I was progressing with the Drillers. I had become a regular starter, and there was talk of moving me up to play for the Rangers. Of course this would mean that we would have to move to Texas, but we were both fine with that, since it meant I would be in the Majors, and Lisa was originally from a small town outside of Dallas called Flower Mound.

Just Believe

Things were going very well for us. We were very happy and loved our lives.

I was out of town playing baseball with the team when I got a call from Lisa's friend Deb. Deb was one of the members of the gym, and she and Lisa had become fast friends.

"Stanley, this is Deb," she said. "Lisa has some sort of bug and can't keep anything down. I am going to take her to the doctor."

"Let me talk with her," I said.

"Well, that might be kind of hard. She has her head in a toilet right now," Deb replied.

I was upset. Lisa is a very healthy person and hardly ever gets sick.

"I'm coming home. I can rent a car and be there in four hours," I told Deb.

"No, you stay there and play the game. I'll call you as soon as we find out what's going on."

I stayed and played the game. It was one of the worst games I had ever played. The coach pulled me aside after the 4th inning to ask me what was going on.

"My wife is sick and I need to go be with her," I told him.

"There is nothing you can do about it from here," he said. "She is going to be fine. Just get your head back in the game. We need you."

I played the rest of the game and then called Deb.

"What's going on? How is she doing?" I asked frantically.

Lisa

Deb snickered for a second and then said, "I think you need to talk to your wife." She handed the phone to Lisa.

"Stanley, honey," she said.

"Yes, Lisa. What is it? Are you OK? I am worried!" I told her.

"Don't worry honey. Everything is fine," Lisa reassured me.

"Oh, thank God. So, what was wrong?" I asked.

"Stanley, are you sitting down?" I didn't say anything. "Stan, you're going to be a daddy..."

I was shell-shocked. I didn't know what to say. How could this be? We had not planned on this yet. We had our goals and our plans and now, a baby?

I sat down on the bench in the locker room and started to cry. I was so happy. This is the second moment in my life that is etched in my memory.

Chapter Two

Change of Plans

"A baby is God's opinion that the world should go on."

Carl Sandburg

So now Lisa was pregnant. My baseball career was going strong. Life was good. At eight weeks pregnant, she was just starting to get a little baby bump and looking so cute. She had planned to keep working up until the baby was born and then stay home with him or her after the birth.

It was looking more and more like I was going to get called up to the Rangers. My coach told me it might be a good idea for me to make some plans and start looking at places to live in the Dallas area. I was very excited.

Lisa's parents were in town for a visit, and we had just finished a nice meal. Lisa's father and I sat outside on the porch and watched the sunset. We talked about life and our future plans. He was excited that we were looking to move to the Dallas area. That would bring us within about 20 miles from them.

Just Believe

That night while we were sleeping, Lisa woke up with bad stomach cramps. We thought maybe it might have been something she ate. I told her I wanted to take her to the emergency room. She didn't want to make a big deal out of it.

She got up to go to the bathroom. When she did, I noticed a spot of blood on the sheet.

"That's it. We're going to the ER," I said.

She conceded, and we took off. I woke her parents up and they quickly got dressed and came with us.

When we got to the hospital, the cramps had increased, and I could tell she was in a lot of pain. They took her to an examining room and the doctor came in to examine her. They made all of us leave the room. I fought to stay in the room with her, but they were adamant that I go. They said it would cause her too much stress and that I needed to leave.

I hated to leave her. They put us in a waiting room that was maybe ten by ten feet. I think it might have been the old smokers' lounge, because it still had a lingering smell of old tobacco. There were a couple of chairs and an old, scratchy couch.

I couldn't sit. I paced back and forth while we waited. We were in the room for about two hours, and I couldn't take it any more. I went to the nurses' station several times.

"What is happening with my wife? Can someone tell me what is going on?" I kept asking.

"Sir, we will let you know when we find out. I am sure she is fine," is all I would get from them.

It was very frustrating.

After being in the room for about two hours, the doctor came in to update us.

"Mr. Walters, I am Doctor Lee," He said.

I could only stare at him as he talked to me.

"I am sorry to say that we were not able to stop the bleeding," the doctor continued.

I felt as though I were 100 miles away, trying to understand what he was saying. He kept talking to me, and I was trying to pay attention to him, but all I heard were the words bleeding and miscarriage. Lisa's father stepped in and started talking with the doctor. I just continued to stare off in the distance. Then the doctor said I could see her. At that, I snapped to and headed down the hallway.

A nurse came alongside of me and directed me to the right room.

As I entered the room, Lisa just looked at me and started to cry.

"I'm sorry, honey," is all she could say.

Sorry! How could she be sorry? This wasn't her fault. I went to her, held her close, and we both cried together. This is the third memory that will always be etched in my mind.

The doctors were not concerned with Lisa's health after the miscarriage. They told us that this happens and that we should keep on trying. So we did. It was not so much that we wanted a kid, or that we were ready for one, but once we were pregnant, we were looking forward to it and really wanted to have a child. We kept on trying. The doctors put her on all kinds of pills and treatments. Over the next two years, Lisa had two more miscarriages. At this point, we resigned ourselves to the fact that we were not going to be able to have children.

During all of this, my life had taken an unexpected turn. Just after the first miscarriage, I was out of town playing a ball game against the Springfield Cardinals. It was a typical summer day. It was hot. If I remember correctly, it was in the upper 90s. I was glad to be playing this game because when we finished, we would get back on the bus headed home. I would have four days without a game, and Lisa and I had planned to take some time and go to a nice little cabin at the Burnt Cabin Marina on Lake Tenkiller. Tenkiller is a beautiful lake in southern Oklahoma that has warm, aqua-blue water. This is one of our favorite places to escape to, and I was really looking forward to the upcoming long weekend.

The score was 10-3. We were up by seven. Winning this game would secure us the top position in the league, so we were all pumped as we were going into the ninth inning. I was in the field at my regular position of shortstop. The batter got up to the plate and squared off. I had taken balls from this guy many times throughout the season. I knew he would swing too hard and top the ball. He would ground it right at me or between the second baseman and me.

I called out to Franky, the second baseman, "Get ready, Franky! This one is going to come to me, and I am going to throw it to you. Runner's out, and we go home!"

Franky gave me a nod, and he moved a couple of steps off the base toward me. The pitcher looked over to me and gave me a nod. We all knew the ball was coming to me.

The pitcher settled in and got into his wind-up. He purposefully threw the batter a fastball to the inside, because he knew this guy would swing at anything. He was right. The batter reared back and swung the bat as hard as he could, driving the ball hard on the ground. I could tell the ball was going to go right between me and second base. I have seen this scenario a thousand times. I have practiced this play since I was in Little League. This play was no different than all those other times except, for some reason, my left knee didn't like it this time.

As the ball came off the bat, I did what I always do. I shifted my weight and dug in. I pivoted on my left leg and started to take off toward the ball. But for some reason, this time was different. This time, my left knee gave out. I can still hear the sound—CRACK or POP. It was kind of a combination of the two. My knee gave way, and I went down like a bag of potatoes.

At first, I didn't realize what had happened. I tried to get up, but I couldn't. I could see the ball going into the outfield and I was frustrated. I tried to get up again, and then all of a sudden the pain hit me. Pain shot up my leg from my knee. When I looked down I could see my leg was bending the wrong way. What was going on?

Then I could hear Franky talking to me. "Just stay down, man. Let's get the doc out here."

Stay down? I can't stay down. I have a game to play. Then the reality of the situation hit me. My knee. Not my *knee*. I have to be healthy to play for the Rangers. This can't be happening.

They got me to the Springfield hospital and took x-rays. I had torn my anterior cruciate ligament (ACL). This ligament in the knee crosses from the underside of the femur (the thigh bone) to the top of the tibia (the bigger bone in the lower leg). It would require surgery and many years of rehab. Even with that, there was no guarantee that I would be able to play at full capacity. My baseball career was all but over.

They patched me up at the hospital. By the time I was ready to go, Lisa had made the three-hour drive from Tulsa to come be with me.

"How are you?" she asked.

"Well, it looks like you married a cripple, and you will have to take care of me for the rest of your life," I replied.

She smiled and came over to the bed and sat next to me. She took my hand in hers.

"Stanley, we are going to be fine. We have gotten through tougher times than this. You can get your surgery, get healed up, and play again," she said reassuringly.

"It's not that easy," I told her. "It takes months, even years, to heal up, and then you are never the same. I'm done, cooked, fried. You name it; I'm it," I said.

She just looked at me and smiled. I wasn't sure what she was up to, but I knew there was something.

"You seem to be taking this pretty well," I said.

She motioned for me to move over in the bed, and she slid in next to me and laid her head on my chest.

Change of Plans

"Stanley," she cooed softly. "What would you say if I told you that there is going to be a big change in our lives?"

Had she not been listening? That is what I was trying to tell her. My career was over and she didn't seem to care or notice. I sat up in bed, which caused her to sit up too.

"Lisa, aren't you listening to me? That is what I am trying to tell you. My days of playing ball are over. I am going to have to find another job. Pro ball is gone," I explained.

She just kept looking at me with this sheepish grin on her face. It was actually starting to make me mad. She didn't see the real issue here, and she was making light of me losing my dream of being a professional ball player.

"Listen," I said. "If you have something to say, you better say it, or I'm not sure what I am going to do next," I replied.

"Stanley, stop. You're going to ruin the moment," Lisa said.

"What moment?" I let out.

"The moment I tell you that you are going to be a daddy," she said smiling.

BAM. Those words hit me like a ton of bricks. Daddy? How? Who? What? I was full of questions. She just looked into my eyes with that angelic smile of hers for what seemed to be hours.

"How can I be a daddy?" I asked her.

"I don't know honey. All I know is that I am pregnant, and you are the daddy."

Just Believe

We both let out a laugh when she said that. I grabbed her around the neck and held her tight. At that moment I knew that being a daddy was more important to me than playing professional baseball.

This is the fourth memory that is etched into my brain.

On the way back to Tulsa, we talked about many different things. She told me of the homeopathic herbs she had been taking to help her get and stay pregnant. I had known that she was seeing a different doctor, but I did not know the details of what she was doing. This was an alternative medicine that uses herbs along with chiropractic care to get and keep the back in alignment so the nerves can do all the work they were made to do. She had been seeing this new doctor for about a year now, and here she was pregnant. She was going to keep on the regimen during the pregnancy.

Listening to her talk took me back to that first time I met her when we went to the little coffee shop. She talked on and on for hours. I loved just sitting and listening to her. She was my angel and I loved her. Now she was going to give me the best gift of all, my son.

Chapter Three

Eddy

"When the going gets tough, the tough get going."
English Proverb

My dad always said to me, "Life is what you make of it." Growing up, I didn't really understand what he meant by that. It wasn't until I got married, and we ran into some of the struggles we did, that I got a good understanding of that phrase. Losing the babies and injuring my knee were some pretty big setbacks. To be honest, there were a couple of times when I wasn't sure what we were going to do. For us, we just kept moving forward. We just kept doing what we knew to do each day, and it all seemed to work out.

I had surgery on my knee right away and started my rehab. Knowing that a pro career was not really an option any more, I went back to my second love, writing. Writing was my minor in college, and I had always loved the art of storytelling, so I started working on my first novel. It was tough. I wrote every day while I was healing up after the surgery.

Just Believe

Lisa was getting bigger and bigger. There is a special kind of beauty that only pregnant women have. I am not sure what it is, but Lisa was more beautiful when she was pregnant than she had ever been before. She would catch me looking at her and get upset with me.

"Stop staring at me," she would say.

"Why? You are beautiful," I would reply.

"I'm fat. My legs are swollen, and my butt is huge," she would complain. I would just laugh at her.

"Yes. All that may be true, honey, but you're my beautiful fat girl with swollen legs and a huge butt, and I love you," I would tease.

She would just wave an arm at me and tell me to stop.

I continued to write until I finished my first book, *The Player*. It was about an old washed-up baseball player that comes out of retirement to help his team win a championship. I guess, in a way, it was about me and my dreams. I started sending it around to different publishers hoping it would get picked up and published.

Lisa carried the baby to full term and gave birth to a beautiful baby boy. We named him Edward after her grandfather. He became Eddy to all who knew and loved him. He was amazing. He had a full head of hair with bright blue eyes.

I still had a pretty strong limp in my left leg as I carried him around the hospital. One of the nurses stopped me and gave me a cart. I think she was afraid I would drop him with my bad knee. She said it was for insurance reasons. I didn't care. I was going to show my boy to anyone and everyone who was willing to look.

Eddy

We brought him home and started our life with a child. I continued to try to get my book published but there were no takers. It was becoming very apparent to me that I would need to do something to make some money. The insurance from my injury covered most of the medical expenses, but there was no regular money coming in other than what Lisa made at the gym.

Now we had little Eddy home, and she wasn't able to work, so I had to get something done. I got online and started looking at all of the want ads. There wasn't very much available for a washed-up ball player. I did, however, find an ad from Globe Publishing for a technical writer. I went in to the office and met with Joel Nelson.

Joel was second generation in the business, and I could tell he really enjoyed the work. He explained the job and what the responsibilities would be.

"You would be hired to write manuals for different products our customers build. You will have to get an understanding of how they are made, how they work, and how to maintain them," he said.

It wasn't fiction, but it was a writing job.

"Do you think you can do that?" he asked.

"Yes, sir, I can," I answered. And that is how I became a technical writer. Not the most exciting thing in the world, but I was gainfully employed. Of course, I also brought my novel and ask Joel to read it. He said he would, and that he would let me know what he thought.

Lisa and I celebrated that night with a nice candlelit dinner for two. Well, two and one-half actually. Eddy enjoyed a nice bottle of formula.

Chapter Four

The Early Years

"A happy family is but an earlier heaven."
John Bowring

Life moved quickly after that point. After three months at home with Eddy, Lisa decided to go back to work at the gym. They were happy to have her come back. Her clientele quickly filled her schedule, and she was working full time. I was able to work from home, so I could watch Eddy and continued to write for Globe. I quickly moved up the ranks to one of their top writers. I had as much work as I could handle.

One day, I stopped by the local pet store on a whim. The humane society was there with several different kinds of pets to adopt. Eddy was just a toddler and loved dogs.

There was one particular little puppy that looked like a Lab-Rottweiler mix. The attendant told us a whole litter had been brought in and dropped off. This was the runt of the litter and the last to go.

Just Believe

I looked at Eddy sitting there with this little puppy licking his face. That was all it took for me. I picked up the puppy and took him home.

That was a pretty good ploy on the part of the pet store. Not being a pet owner, I had to then purchase the necessary puppy supplies needed to take care of our newest family member. Now all I had to do was convince Lisa this was a good idea.

She came home, and I had dinner made. I cooked my traditional "will you forgive me" meal of spaghetti. The truth is, it is the only thing that I know how to cook. When she walked in the door, she knew something was up.

"OK, what did you do?" she said as she set her keys on the table by the door.

"Whatever do you mean?" I came back at her.

"You're cooking. That means you did something wrong, and you want to make it up to me."

She had a huge smile on her face, and I couldn't help but laugh at the situation.

"Am I that transparent? OK, you got me." I wiped my hands off on my apron and walked over to the pantry. "Come here," I said.

Lisa walked over as I opened the door. She could see Eddy sitting on the floor playing with the new puppy. Lisa smiled big and looked at me with this *Now you did it* look on her face. She bent down, and the puppy came running over to her and started biting on her hands and growling. Lisa was in love. Eddy was watching her and then he just blurted out "COOPER." We looked at each other, not really knowing where this came from, but from that moment on the puppy was known as Cooper.

Time continued to fly by. Before we knew it, Eddy was walking and talking.

On his fourth birthday, I got him a junior-sized baseball glove. We started to play catch all the time.

At six, I signed him up for a Little League T-ball team. It was great. The field was just down the road from our house. Eventually, I became the coach of the team.

As Eddy grew older, he seemed to develop his arm. He liked to throw the ball, and he had a pretty strong arm for his age. I started working with him as a pitcher.

By age eight, he was working out his curveball and a strong knuckleball. I think his love for baseball was as strong as mine. If we were not at the practice field, we were in the front yard throwing the ball. I think sometimes Lisa felt a little left out. Lucky for us, she liked to read, so when we were playing catch, she would be sitting on the porch with Cooper reading.

Eddy was now ten years old. Lisa was never able to conceive another child, and we had come to the point of accepting this. We were very happy with our small family and really didn't feel the need for another child though I think deep down, Lisa would have liked to have another child, maybe a little girl for her to play with. She says she is fine, but I can tell there are times when she feels that she has failed me.

I think it is hard for a woman not to be able to bear children. Much like a man who has lost his job. As a man, you have this instinct to provide for your family. When you cannot do that, you lose contact with who you are and you feel lost. I think Lisa feels that way sometimes. I have told her that I am fine with everything, and that I love her no matter what. More children or not, I am happy with our situation. She says she believes me, and that she is happy too, but deep down I believe she wanted more kids.

Life was good and only seemed like it was going to get better. Nothing could have prepared me for what was about to happen.

Chapter Five

Eddy's Birthday

*"Children are the hands by which we
take hold of heaven."*
Henry Ward Beecher

It was springtime in Tulsa. This is my favorite time of year. Not only because it is the beginning of baseball season, but it is a time of new things. The trees were in full bud. The flowers were in full bloom. The air was warm, and it was Eddy's birthday. This was a big day at the Walters home. Not only because he was our only son, but he was also the only grandchild on either side of the family. For some reason, Steven couldn't find a girl that would marry him, so Eddy reigned supreme as the number one grandchild. He loved every minute of it.

He also took advantage of every minute of it. He knew how to turn on the puppy-dog eyes and get either set of his grandparents to do whatever his little heart desired. Lisa would get on him about it. She could see how he sweetly manipulated them.

Just Believe

"Lisa," her mother would say, "leave him alone. I am fully aware of what the little dickens is up to. We love every minute of it, so you just let your father and me be grandparents and spoil our little angel."

Lisa would just shake her head and walk away. Her mother loved to dote on Eddy, and Eddy loved to be doted on. My parents were no different. I can remember times when they would be running all over town to take Eddy to the movie he wanted, then the restaurant he wanted, and then to the store to buy the toy he wanted. They loved every moment and would not have changed it.

We celebrated Eddy's birthday on a Saturday. All of the family had come to join us—Lisa's parents from Texas and mine from just down the road. Steven came in from Oklahoma City. He had gotten a job as an anesthesiologist. He was a pretty good ball player, but it turned out he was actually pretty smart. He loved what he did, and had started looking into transferring to Tulsa so he could be closer to us. Since he had never married and never had kids of his own, Eddy had become kind of a surrogate son for him.

The house was abuzz with people. Since I had become the coach of Eddy's team, we had made a lot of friends in the area. I loved coaching, and I was able to get good results out of my kids.

We must have had 50 people crammed into our little house. We moved into this house when Eddy turned two. We just needed more room. The house was in the older, historic part of town. It was built around 1920 and was actually on the historical homes list with the historical society. It had a great layout that worked well for our family.

The house was on a corner lot and had a detached garage with a nice-sized back and front yard. The house was all one level though it had a basement. This is rare for houses in the South. You couldn't live in it. We just used it for storage. There were three bedrooms that ran along the south side of the house. We converted the front bedroom into my office. This is where I worked on my writing. The middle bedroom belonged to Lisa and me. The back, smallest bedroom was Eddy's. The kitchen had been updated when we bought it. It had nice, stainless steel appliances and a huge, granite center island. The middle of the house was a full-sized dining room, and the living room was at the front of the house. My favorite feature of the house was the covered porch that went along the front of the house and continued over the driveway to create a nice carport. This comes in handy on the hot Tulsa summers.

All the guests had arrived, and we were all spread throughout the dining room and living room. Lisa's dad was at his station on the porch in the rocking chair. Lisa had made a birthday cake in the shape of a baseball diamond.

We all gathered in the dining room to sing *Happy Birthday*. It was a great day. I was especially excited because I had a very special gift for Eddy. I had purchased the Cadillac of baseball gloves—the Rawlings QS435. This was the king of all gloves, and by the price you would think it was lined with gold. Eddy had wanted one of these for a long time, and I had kept putting it off because I wanted to get it for his birthday. I think I was more excited to give it to him than he was going to be to get it.

We sang *Happy Birthday*, and he blew out all but two of the candles. One of the kids from his team quickly yelled, "You have two girlfriends, Eddy!"

"No, I don't," he snipped back at him.

"All right, all right. That's enough," I said. "If Eddy doesn't want to tell us about his girlfriends, then we will just let him keep his secret," I teased.

"Dad, I don't have any girlfriends. Stop it!" Eddy protested.

Lisa jumped in. She wanted to move on with the party. "You two knock it off. I will separate you if I have to," she warned.

After cutting the cake, it was present time, and I could hardly wait. Eddy got all kinds of presents from his friends. His grandparents got him a new MX bike that he had been wanting. Most of the other gifts Eddy received had something to do with baseball. He was pulling in quite the haul. I was impressed. I don't remember birthdays with this many gifts when I was a kid.

I let all his friends give their presents. I wanted to save mine for last. I wanted the big reveal effect.

When he had opened the last of the presents, he looked at me with his *I know there is one more Dad, and I think I know what it is* look. I had to play it out a little. I couldn't give in so easy.

"Well, let's get this mess cleaned up," I said. Eddy just sat there looking at me. "Dad, are you forgetting something?" he asked expectantly.

"Uh, no, I don't think so. Come on now. Let's get this mess cleaned up," I replied, trying to distract him. He wouldn't hear of it.

"Come on, Dad. I know you got me something. You have been hiding it under your bed for a month," he said mischievously.

"What? How do you know that?" I asked, quite surprised that he had discovered my hiding place.

"It's been kind of hard not to notice. You keep taking it out and looking at it," he said.

Well, he had me there. I guess I was a bigger kid than he was.

"All right. You got me," I admitted.

I went in the other room and came out with the nicely-wrapped present. He dug into it with an anticipation that you could almost feel. Then he pulled it out as if he were a pirate opening a treasure chest filled with gold and jewels. He held the glove high in the air. All his baseball friends cheered. He ran over to me and jumped in my arms.

"Thank you, Dad! You're the best," he cheered.

"I love you, son. Now go play," I beamed.

He ran out to the front yard to play with his friends.

The day wound down and people started to leave. The day had been full of cake, ice cream, and presents. Everyone had a great time. The party had finally come to a close, and everyone had left except our parents and Steven.

The girls were in the kitchen cleaning up as the guys sat out on the porch watching Eddy ride his new bike up and down the driveway. It seemed funny to me that he was still using training wheels. As athletic as he was, he still lacked the confidence to try to ride without them. It was a perfect end to a perfect day. We sat on the porch until dark.

My parents went home, and Lisa's parents and brother went to their hotel. Eddy fell asleep in a chair in the living room with his new glove in hand. I had to carry him to his bed. He was totally exhausted from the events of the day. That night, Lisa and I quickly fell asleep.

The next day, Lisa had a couple of clients to meet with in the afternoon. Since it was Sunday, Eddy and I planned to hang out around the house and play with all of his new toys. We played catch out in the front yard for a while, and then Eddy made an announcement.

"Dad, I think I am ready to ride my bike without training wheels," he said confidently.

"Are you sure son?" I asked.

"Yeah. I am the only kid on my team that still has training wheels. I feel like a dork," Eddy admitted sheepishly. I had to let out a chuckle.

"Well, if you're sure, let's take them off," I agreed.

We went around the back of the house to the garage. I opened the garage door and went to my workbench on the left side to find a wrench.

Eddy's Birthday

"Dad? When are you going to clean out this garage?" Eddy wondered aloud.

The garage was kind of a mess. We had not been able to park a car in it for years. There were boxes full of stuff from years past. I collected newspapers for recycling and just hadn't gotten around to banding them and putting them out. There was still some room in the middle, but it seemed as each year went by, it got fuller and fuller. This had been a point of conversation between Lisa and me. It was always one of those "I'll get around to it" things that I just never got around to doing.

"Uh, how about we make that our summer project? You and me tackling this garage and getting it cleaned out for Mom. She would love that," I said.

"Yeah, let's do it," he replied. "That would be fun."

"OK," I said. "It's a deal. We will get those training wheels off and, starting tomorrow, we will start cleaning the garage."

"Deal," he said.

We found the wrenches and walked the bike from the driveway to under the porch covering. I took off the training wheels one at a time. Then, for a little drama, I threw them over my shoulder to the ground. Eddy just giggled. He was so excited to finally try this. He hopped up on the bike. I walked with him as he tried to balance on the bike. With my hand on his shoulder, Eddy pedaled down to the garage and turned around back toward the street. He was starting to get the hang of it.

"Let me go, Dad," he yelled.

"Not yet, son," I said. "Let's keep working on this before you go out on your own."

We reached the street, turned around, and headed back to the garage. He was doing well.

"Let me go. Let me go! I want to do it on my own," he yelled impatiently.

"OK," I replied. "Just hang on a sec. I want to get turned around so you have the whole driveway."

We turned around at the garage and headed toward the front of the house. He got up on the pedals and started to push hard

"OK. Now, Dad, let me go," Eddy pleaded excitedly.

"OK. Just go slow. Make sure you stop at the end of the driveway." I said.

"OK. OK, let me go, Dad"

By this time I was walking briskly alongside him.

"Here you go," I encouraged as I let go.

I stood watching Eddy cruising along the driveway. He was doing well. A little shaky, but he was doing it. I was so proud.

Then I heard it. A sound that I will never forget 'til the day I die. The sound that changed my life forever. It was the sound of a diesel engine in a delivery truck gaining speed.

I looked over to my right, and down the street I could see a truck rounding the corner. I looked back at Eddy, and I realized that he didn't see the truck and wasn't slowing down or stopping. He was headed right for the street.

Eddy's Birthday

Everything kicked into slow motion. I couldn't yell. I could hardly move. I was frozen with fear where I stood as Eddy steadily cruised down the driveway toward the street. The truck kept coming and was still gaining speed.

I finally found my voice and yelled out to him, "EDDY, STOP!"

I yelled and yelled, but he didn't hear me. Eddy was caught up in the moment. I started to run towards him just as he reached the sidewalk.

"EDDY! EDDY, STOP!"

The truck continued gaining speed. As I ran towards Eddy, I can remember thinking to myself, *What is that driver doing going so fast on this street? We need to get signs, or a speed bump, or something.*

Everything around me was moving in slow motion except Eddy. He was speeding toward the street, and he wouldn't listen to me. I was running as fast as I could, but it felt like I was crawling.

Eddy had crossed the sidewalk and reached the street. He zipped onto the pavement, entering the street just behind our parked car.

I realized immediately that the car would block the truck driver's view of Eddy. He was just a few yards out of reach when he looked over his shoulder and saw me chasing after him. He had a puzzled look on his face. Then he heard the noise, too. He looked up the street and saw the truck, but by that time, it was too late to slow down or stop.

He looked back at me. He didn't have to say anything. His eyes said it all. *Help me, Dad*! they cried out to me.

Just Believe

As Eddy cleared our parked car, the truck driver finally saw him. He tried to stop. He hit the brakes and swerved hard to his right, but it didn't matter. Eddy was in the middle of street by that time. The truck hit him just before my hand reached the back seat of his bike.

At that moment, everything froze. I had so much forward momentum from running, I actually ran into the truck and was thrown back into the street. I hit my head on the street and was dazed. I don't think I actually lost consciousness, but I was in a daze. All sound felt as if it was coming from miles away. My vision was cloudy and overexposed.

I slowly came to and frantically looked around for Eddy. I finally saw him. He was lying in the street. He did not respond when I called his name. I crawled over to him and held his head in my lap. It looked like he was sleeping. As I held him, the past 7 years played in my head. I felt as though I sat there for hours, though I know it was only a few minutes. I don't remember anything after that, just that I died that day, too.

That is moment number five that is etched in my memory.

The next few days were a blur. No one prepares you for the loss of a child. How can they? No one should ever have to go through that. Lisa tried to console me, but I wouldn't have any of it. How could she be nice to me? I killed her child.

"Stanley, it was an accident," she would say to me.

Like that is supposed to make it better. I was the ultimate loser, and she was married to me. We held a funeral two days later. Eddy's casket was closed because of the extent of his injuries. Just another reminder of what I did to him.

I remember standing at the graveside, just staring at the picture of Eddy perched near the coffin. My father was standing behind me. He didn't say a word to me. He didn't have to. I knew what he was thinking. *How could you let this happen? I wish it was you instead of him.* He stood behind me judging me. They were all judging me.

Everyone who gathered to mourn Eddy looked at me with those pathetic looks on their faces. They would say things like, "There was no one like him," or "Try to remember the time you had with him and celebrate that." What is that supposed to mean? Say what you *mean*!

You're an idiot, and you killed your son.

We all know they meant well, but at the time there was nothing they could have said to make any of it better. I hated my life and myself.

After the funeral was over, we held a reception at the house. I still don't know why we did that. All I could think about was that just four days earlier we were all there celebrating his birthday. Now we were celebrating his death.

I couldn't talk to anyone, so I just sat outside on the porch by myself with Cooper. He seemed to be the only one that understood me.

Chapter Six

An Unexpected Guest

"When one door closes, another opens; but we often look so long and so regretfully upon the closed door that we do not see the one which has opened for us."

Alexander Graham Bell

Two years after the accident, I had become a shell of the man I was. I wasn't able to let go of what happened to Eddy. My heart was empty and lifeless. For the first six months or so after the accident, Lisa tried to reach out to me. She would sit with me and try to get me to talk to her.

"There is nothing to say. I killed our son. What else do you need to know?" I would bitterly reply.

Eventually Lisa just gave up. She filled her days with her work and was gone from the house as much as she could be. I tried to work but couldn't keep a clear train of thought. I made a few big mistakes on a couple of jobs and was demoted to a copy editor. I was now proofreading other people's work. Most days, I just stared at my screen.

After Eddy's death, my publisher offered to publish my book if I would make some changes to it. I think he did this out of pity for me. He was still waiting for the changes he ordered. The days were starting to bleed into each other. I had no sense of direction.

About two weeks after the accident, I moved into Eddy's room. I just couldn't sleep with Lisa anymore. I felt so guilty. I wanted to be close to him. I wanted to smell his smell. I wanted to see his picture.

Lisa still asked me to come back to our room. To be honest, I am not sure why she stayed with me. I would have left a long time ago.

I dreamed of the accident almost every night. It haunted me and wouldn't let me go. I got up every morning and did just about the same thing every day. Lisa was usually gone off to work by the time I got up. I would get a cup of coffee and go into my office to do some work. When I got in there, I would be faced with that evil little red blinking light on the answering machine. It was the same thing every time.

"Mr. Walters your house payment is late," or "Mr. Walters we are going to be forced to put your account into collections." They really should work on being more creative with their messages.

I would erase them and turn to my computer to work, but when I started to write, nothing would make any sense. Everything I wrote seemed like gibberish.

Eventually, I would delete everything and take Cooper for a walk.

Cooper was my constant companion through this whole thing. Cooper didn't judge me; he accepted me for the pitiful man that I was.

An older, African-American woman moved into the house next door. Her name was Miss Esther. I'm not sure why she called herself *Miss* Esther, and not just Esther, but I didn't really care. She was a foster parent and had four kids living with her: two girls and two boys. One of the younger boys was in a wheelchair. I didn't know all of their names, and I really didn't plan to get to know them. I figured that most of the time foster kids are trouble. There is a reason no one wants them. I made sure to lock my doors at night and to lock the garage too. One day I couldn't find my air pump, and I was pretty convinced one of them took it.

I took Cooper for a walk down by the ball field. It was the same field where I used to coach Eddy's baseball team. The field is now in rough shape. When I was the coach, I used to make sure they took good care of it. There was grass growing in the baselines, and the weeds were growing tall along the back fence. There was an old bleacher set up behind the outfield fence, just off the right field. I liked to go there and sit and watch the kids practice.

They had a new coach. I think he was a father to one of the kids on the team. He really had no clue what he was doing. It frustrated me to see him try to coach the kids.

Just Believe

I was sitting on the bench at the back of the field with Cooper when an older man dressed in a maintenance uniform walked up to us. He introduced himself as Sam. I wasn't really in the mood to chitchat with this guy, but he kept asking me questions.

"Which one?" he inquired.

"Which one *what*?" I replied.

"Kid. Which kid is yours?" he clarified.

Why would he think that I have a kid? Why would you just walk up to someone and ask a question like that?

"None of them. I don't have any kids," I told him.

I tried to end the conversation there, but I couldn't help my outburst when I saw the coach of the baseball team giving the pitcher some very wrong advice about how he was throwing. I made a comment about it, and Sam laughed.

"That's Josh; *she* has a great arm all right," he chuckled.

She? As I watched her, she took her hat off and revealed a head of long hair tucked up into her hat.

"Oh, I see," I said, a bit surprised.

"She is one of Miss Esther's kids," he said.

"Really? You better keep your eye on her then. I think one of those kids stole my air pump," I cautioned.

Sam just smiled and kept watching the practice. I watched the kids a little longer and then got up and left.

"I'll see you later," Sam said. I just kept walking. *I don't need any new friends,* I thought to myself.

For some reason, the next few days were very tough. Lisa was on me about work and getting money into the house. My publisher was asking for new pages on the book, or he was going to need the advance he paid me back. The kids next door were loud and woke me up at the break of dawn. Everything seemed to irritate me more than usual.

Lisa made me dinner, and I went to the kitchen to eat. She started at me about cleaning the garage out again. Something about her friend Deb having a garage sale and wanting to get rid of some stuff.

"Fine," is all I said.

I guess that wasn't good enough for her. Then she started in on me about my book.

"Did you make any progress on your book today?" she inquired.

That just sent me over the edge.

"Why do you have to nag me all the time?" I retorted.

"I'm not nagging. I just want to have a little conversation with you," she said.

"OK, fine. Talk. Come on, *talk*!" I replied.

I shut her down again just like I had done so many times over the previous two years. What was I doing? Why did I hate her? *Did* I hate her? I didn't know what I felt or why I felt it. I guess the real question here was how could she love me? I didn't know what to do so I just got up and left. I left her wounded and hurting. It seemed that all I could do at that time in my life was hurt.

That night, I dreamed of Eddy again. It always started out the same way. We were laughing and having a good time outside the house. I take off the training wheels, and he climbs on the bike. Then I push him off, and he rides the bike out into the street. There is a horrible noise, and I wake up in a cold sweat.

This time I woke up at 6:00 A.M. I got up and decided to tackle the garage. I walked out wearing the old sweatpants and ratty T-shirt that I slept in. When I opened the door, I was greeted with a wall of boxes and junk. I had newspapers piled up from the past five years. When I looked at the garage, all I could think was that my life was pretty much the same: filled with junk that I didn't want but also didn't know what to do with. I hated that place.

As I was working on the garage, I saw Lisa walk out of the house to our SUV with a box in her hands. She didn't say anything.She didn't even look at me. I was sure she was still upset with me for yelling at her last night.

I continued to work on the garage for another couple of hours. I was surprised by all of the stuff that we had accumulated in our lives. Stuff that we didn't use or need for that matter. But for some reason we kept it. I needed to take a break and try to clear my head a little so I went back to my office to grab my coffee cup.

As I walked back to the kitchen, I passed Eddy's room. I noticed something different in there. For some reason, Lisa made my bed that morning, but that's not all. One of the dresser drawers was left open. The dresser had not been touched since the accident. It still had all of Eddy's things in it. Why would that drawer be open?

I walked in to check it out. The drawer was empty. All of Eddy's shirts were missing. What did she do with them? I checked the other drawers. His shorts and pants were gone, too. Even his hats were gone. All that was left was one of Eddy's stuffed animals. It was the spotted dog that I had got him at the State Fair.

How could she do this? I wasn't sure what to do. I was so angry I was afraid if I saw her right then I would explode. I grabbed Cooper and went for a walk. I had to release some of the steam.

Lisa was gone for most of the day. I was not able to work on the garage any more. I was not able to concentrate on anything other than what she did with those clothes.

At 6:00 P.M., she pulled into the driveway. I watched her through the window. She got out of the car and looked down at the garage. I realized then that I left the door open and boxes all over the driveway. She got a look of disappointment on her face that I had seen so many times since Eddy's death. She came toward the house. I was not sure what I was going to say or how I was going to say it. I just knew that I was going to let her have it.

She walked past our sidewalk and continued down the street. She had something in her hand that I couldn't quite make out. I continued to watch her as she went up the walk to our neighbor's house. Why is she going to see Miss Esther? What would she need to talk with her about? I continued to watch her as she talked with Miss Esther at the door. Then she turned and started walking back toward our house. I wasn't sure what to do, so I sat in a chair.

She opened the door slowly. I guess she was hoping I would be asleep so she could sneak in the house without waking me. She still had something in her hands. It looked like an old brass oil lamp. *What would she be doing with that?* I wondered. She set the lamp down on the coffee table and looked at me. She knew she was in trouble.

"So, where have you been all day?" I demanded. She looked at me as if she were a young schoolgirl getting yelled at by her father.

"I was at the garage sale. I told you," she replied.

"I was in Eddy's room today," I began. She knew what I was talking about. "Just who do you think you are? What did you do with it?" I barked.

She didn't answer me. She just looked away.

"Answer me! What did you do with his stuff?" I asked angrily.

"I just thought we could put it to good use," she said quietly.

"How could you do that?" I blurted out.

"Do what, Stanley? Get on with my life?" retorted Lisa.

"Don't start with me!" I said.

"It's been two years," she said.

I couldn't believe what I was hearing.

"Two years? You make it seem like that is a long time," I asserted.

"It is a long time," she replied.

I had to walk around, but I had no place to go, so I just started pacing back and forth. Lisa stood near the couch with her hands held together in front of her.

"How can you be so cold? He was your son, too!" I said. I could tell this cut into her.

"You don't think that I know that? You don't think that I miss him every moment of every day?" she replied.

"You sure don't act like it. You go on as if it never happened." I was still pacing back and forth.

"Stanley, listen to me. It's time to move on," she said.

That stopped me in my tracks. I couldn't look at her I was so upset.

"You had no right...you're just throwing away his memory," I replied.

She slowly sat down on the couch.

"Stanley, I can't do this anymore."

"Do what?" I yelled.

She had finally had it. She blurted out, "This! This constant arguing."

"So now it's my fault. You blame me for all of this," I countered.

"Well, I wasn't the one watching him," she replied.

Those words cut into me like a knife. I had always feared that she blamed me, and now I knew it was true. All the years of her telling me it wasn't my fault and that it was just a terrible accident were all washed away with those words. I was crushed even more than I had ever been.

"I knew it. You blame me. You have always blamed me," I cried.

I turned away from her. Tears of pain were forming in my eyes. I was completely defeated. All I could do was lash out at her.

Just Believe

"No, I'm sorry. I didn't mean to say that," she said softly.

She was trying to help me. Even in these bad times, she was still an angel. I didn't want to hurt her, but the words just started coming out of my mouth.

"Well, it's too late. You said it," I answered.

"Stanley, stop. I didn't mean it," Lisa pleaded.

"You call yourself a mother," I said as I turned around with the most hateful look on my face I can imagine.

Please understand. I did not hate her. I hated myself. I hated what happened, and now I hated what I had become. I even hated the way I was treating her right then. But the words just kept coming out of my mouth.

"Where were you on that day? Why weren't you there to watch him?"

I kept walking toward her, and she backed away from me with every step.

I saw the lamp sitting on the table in the corner of my eye. I reached down and grabbed it. Something had to be hurt right now and the lamp was the closest thing for me to grab.

"And now…now you just take what we have left of him, and you sell it to the highest bidder. Then you come home with this. What is this?" I screamed as I shoved the lamp in her face.

Then I didn't really know what to do, so I threw it into the old fireplace as hard as I could. It crashed into some candles and clay candle stands that Lisa had decorated with. The lamp crashed into all of it with force. Pieces of pottery went everywhere. I turned and stormed out the door. I wasn't sure where I was going. I just knew I needed to leave.

I walked around the neighborhood for about an hour. I had to calm down. I realized that the way our marriage was going was no good for either of us. It was time to end it. I was going to go back to the house to tell her that I was going to leave. I didn't want anything. I didn't deserve anything. She would be better off without me around.

When I got back to the house, I opened the door slowly. This time it was me who wanted to sneak in the house. When I opened the door, I was surprised to see Lisa sitting on the couch looking at the chair as if she were talking with someone. When she heard the door, she turned to look at me.

As I stepped in the door, I said, "What are you doing?"

"Talking with Charles," she said.

Then she turned back to the chair and was totally surprised that there was no one there. She stood up and faced me.

"Stanley, I don't know how to explain this. I was picking up the mess, and I read the side of the old oil lamp. It's hard to see, but etched on its side are the words, "*Just Believe.*" I read it and then said to myself, *I wish I could.* The lamp started vibrating and the light in the ceiling got real bright and then burned out. I heard a knock at the door. There was a man standing outside. He said he came because I asked for him. He gave me a card."

Lisa looked down to the table and reached for a card that was not there. This stumped her. I could tell she thought what she was saying was true, but it made no sense to me.

"So, you're telling me you rubbed the lamp and a genie popped out?" I said sarcastically.

"Not a genie. He said he was a messenger," Lisa explained.

I didn't know what to say. Had this tragic fight caused my wife to go insane? She was telling me that she said *Just Believe* and a genie, I mean messenger, popped out of the lamp. This was all going nowhere fast.

"Listen, Lisa. I can't continue to pretend that everything is going to be OK. I'm going to find an apartment this week. You can have everything. I'm just done."

That was all I could say. She just stared at me. She didn't cry. I honestly think she was relieved in a way. I know I would have been. I was no good for her. I was poison, and I was just getting worse. Being with me had even caused her to hallucinate. Leaving would be for the best.

The next morning I woke up and got out of the house as quick as I could. I did not want to face her after my performance the night before. I took a walk down to the ballpark. I thought I would spend some time alone with Cooper. The neighborhood team was practicing again. The girl from next door, Josh, was pitching. She had a great arm, but she was just throwing the wrong way. As a ball player and former coach, it was frustrating to watch.

Sam came by again, and I am pretty sure he could tell by my body language that I was not in the conversing mindset. This didn't seem to bother him though. He just came right up to me and started talking.

"It looks like you've got a lot on your mind," he said.

"That is an understatement," I replied, hoping he would get the hint and move on.

Just then the coach on the baseball team was instructing one of the kids on how to stand when batting. The coach was doing it all wrong. He had the kid standing with his feet together instead of spread apart, so he could use his body weight to put force behind the swing. I couldn't take it.

"Look at that guy. He has *no idea* what he is doing," I moaned.

Just then, the kid swung the bat backwards into the coach's stomach. He went down like a ton of bricks.

"Bless his heart. He is doing the best he can. They could really use someone who knows what they are doing," said Sam. I knew what he was getting at.

"Me? Not interested. Those days are long gone," I replied.

I was hoping that would shut him up, but he kept on talking.

"They could really use your help. From what I hear, you are quite the coach," Sam continued.

That was enough for me. "I'm not sure what you have heard, but I think you need to drop it," I said firmly.

Sam was undeterred. "Maybe you need them just as much as they need you."

"What makes you think you know what I need?" I replied.

"I'm just saying...maybe this could help you with your loss."

Just Believe

That was it. Who was this guy to talk about Eddy? He didn't know him.

"What do you know about my loss? Have you held your son in your lap...and..." I trailed off. That was all I could say. I had to leave.

"I'm sorry, Stan. I just think that..." he continued.

"Just mind your own business. You don't know me. You don't know what I need. Come on, Coop!"

I stood up and left. Sam just looked at me with pleading eyes. I could tell he wanted to help me, but he didn't know me. He didn't know what I had gone through. The curious thing is that I couldn't figure out how he knew I had lost someone. He must have heard about it through the neighborhood. It was no secret. Everyone in the area was aware of what happened. I just couldn't figure out why he had such an interest in me. It really bugged me.

Before Sam showed up, I had realized that I needed to make some changes. I needed to talk to Lisa and apologize for my behavior the night before. I didn't want to fight anymore. I didn't want to keep being the jerk I was. I still planned to leave and get out of her life, but I didn't want to be a jerk about it. So I decided to head back home, forget about my conversation with the crazy groundskeeper, and apologize to Lisa.

When I walked in the door, she was folding clothes on the couch. The lamp was sitting on the coffee table. She must have spent the morning cleaning up the pieces of broken pottery and candles, because the floor was clean. She had rearranged the display in the fireplace, though it was short a few pieces.

When I entered, all I could say was, "Hey."

Lisa stopped folding clothes and just looked ahead.

"I don't want to fight," I said.

She turned toward me saying, "I don't either."

Then she just started talking. I was surprised. I thought I would have to do all of the talking.

"I know you didn't believe me when I told you about Charles. I didn't really believe it myself. But Miss Esther came by today, and she told me he was for real," Lisa explained.

Miss Esther? What was she talking about? Now Miss Esther was in on the whole genie from the lamp thing? I tried to keep my composure and not yell.

"Lisa, *please.* There is no magic genie that is going to come out of a lamp and make everything all better," I said as patiently as I could.

"But what if it is real? What if he can help us?" she replied.

That was it for me. What kind of garbage did she believe now? I would show her. I grabbed the lamp off of the table.

"You want to know what is real? I'll show you what IS real!"

I stormed out the door and down the driveway. Lisa was following behind, yelling at me to stop. At the end of the driveway stood our two garbage cans that I had set out that morning for the trash man to take. When I got there I grabbed the lid off of one of them and threw the lamp down in the can as hard as I could. Lisa was standing about ten feet from me with a look of bewilderment on her face.

"There is no genie! There is no magic!" I yelled.

I then took off back to the house. She just stared at the can with disbelief. I was going to go to my room to start packing. That was it for me. Now that my wife was crazy, I had to get out of there.

I walked up the stairs, onto the porch, and through the front door. Lisa was following behind me.

As I got to the middle of the room, Cooper barked at me. He was sitting next to the coffee table. On the table was the lamp. I stopped dead in my tracks. I looked at Lisa and she looked at me.

"How did you do that?" I asked.

"What are you talking about?"

I pointed to the lamp sitting on the table. A sense of rage ran through my veins.

"How did you put that lamp on the table?" I demanded.

"Stanley, I don't know how it got there," she said.

I lunged at the table so fast that Cooper jumped back. I grabbed the lamp and headed to the back door. Lisa was on my tail.

"Stanley, please stop. What are you going to do?" she pleaded.

I didn't want to tell her. I just wanted to destroy this thing. It had almost become a symbol of my pain to me. It was something that I didn't understand and something that I couldn't escape. I was going to destroy it once and for all. I burst through the back door and went straight to the garage. I threw the lamp down on the bench and grabbed the biggest hammer I could find. Lisa tried once again to stop me.

"Stanley! Stop! Please honey, stop."

It was too late. I was on a mission and nothing was going to stop me from destroying this thing. I took the hammer and raised my arm as high as I could. I came down hard on the lamp with a blow that had two years of pain behind it. The base of the lamp came flying off of it. I raised my arm again and down I came with a force that I didn't know I had. BAM! The sound of metal on metal rang out as the lamp crumpled under the blow.

Lisa'd had enough. She went back into the house. I was fine with that. I had work to do, and I was almost enjoying it.

Bam, bam, bam! Blow after blow, the lamp was crushed to the point that it was now unrecognizable. It just looked like a hunk of brass that had been run over by a train. After about 15 blows, I finally stopped. I was sweating and breathing hard. My wrist was sore. All of the items on the work bench were scattered about because they bounced every time I hit the lamp. I actually felt better.

I picked up all of the pieces that were left of the lamp and headed into the house. I was going to show her that there was no magic. Nothing could fix us. We were hopeless. I was hopeless. When I entered the kitchen through the back door, Lisa was standing at the sink with her back to the room. I went up to her with a handful of crushed brass pieces.

"Take a good look, Lisa. It's just a hunk of metal," I sneered. She wouldn't look at me.

"You're just mean," is all she could say.

"There is nothing magical about it," I insisted.

As soon as I said that, I heard a noise from behind me. It was kind of a swoosh noise, as if someone had opened the door and the wind had blown in. Then I heard him for the first time.

"Are you sure about that, Stanley?"

I turned around to see an older African-American man dressed in a nice tweed suit. He was just setting his hat down on the center island, and he had a cane in his left hand. I was stunned. I didn't know what to say. I looked down at my hands. The crushed pieces of brass were now the whole oil lamp they were before I attacked it. Out of shock, I dropped the lamp, and it landed on its base.

The old man watched the lamp hit the floor and cringed as it fell. "Careful with that, Stanley. It's an antique."

I didn't know what to say. I looked over at Lisa. She just had a big smile on her face as if to say, *See I'm not crazy.* Charles pushed a chair out from the center island with his foot.

"Stanley, how about you take a seat, and we can have a talk."

I just complied and sat down next to him. I wasn't sure what to think, but I knew something was going on that I needed to listen to.

"What... who... who are you?" is all I could say.

An Unexpected Guest

"Charles Montgomery III, at your service." He reached out his hand to shake mine.

"You really the genie from that lamp?" I asked.

Charles was clearly irritated with the question. "Genie? Let me show you something."

He then took his cane and pointed at our oven door. The glass window on the front became like a TV screen. First there was a little static, and then a picture of a blue man with a turban on his head appeared. It was clear that this was what your stereotypical genie would look like.

"Look here. Genie. Genie." As he said the word *genie*, a different image of another genie would pop up on the screen. "Genie. Genie." I got the message. He wasn't a genie. Then the image disappeared and the oven door transformed back into glass.

Charles grabbed my chin and turned my head so I looked him directly in the eyes.

"Do I look like a genie to you?" he asked.

"Sorry," is all I could say.

"No. I'm sorry. It's just a bit of a sore spot for me. To answer your question, Stanley, I am a messenger. I am here to help you see beyond yourself and your current situation. You are correct, Stanley, there is no magic in the lamp. You see, you can have anything you want in life if you are only willing to first believe. You and Lisa are in a tough spot...mainly because you have lost hope. Right now, you believe that there is no way out other than to give up. Don't feel bad. This happens to a lot of people.

Just Believe

"Many times people get their eyes off of the truth and embrace a lie. Then they begin to believe that lie. In time, this lie becomes their truth, and their whole life is built around it." His statement confused me.

"A lie?"

"Yes. For you, it's the lie that your life ended the day your son died."

That hurt. I looked away for a moment. He stopped talking and gave me a second to reconnect. I looked over at Lisa. She just looked back at me with eyes full of compassion. Then he continued.

"You cannot forgive yourself for this tragic event, so you punish yourself and those around you. The truth, Stanley, is your life *can* and *should* go on. You must let go of the pain and live your life to its fullest."

That just seemed too easy to me. Just let go. Didn't he think that I had tried that?

"That's easy for you to say," I sighed.

"Yes, I guess it is. Because I believe that life should be lived even when a tragic event has occurred."

Charles paused a moment to let this sink in. Then he continued.

"My message is this: You can have anything you want in life, including happiness and forgiveness, if you are willing to just believe you can."

This was too easy for me. Simply believing for something just didn't make sense.

"I think it would have been better if you were a genie. You could grant me three wishes, and I could wish my way out of this," I replied.

That statement amused Charles. He laughed out loud and then got a bit of a grin on his face.

"Well now, that's an interesting idea. Hmm, three wishes. I don't normally do that, but if that helps you, then three wishes it is."

"Let me get this straight. You are going to give me three wishes? I can have anything I want?" I asked.

"Yes, but there will have to be some rules."

Charles reached to his left and grabbed a pair of reading glasses that seemed to come out of thin air. Then he reached over with his right hand and came back with a journal that again appeared to come from nowhere. Lisa and I just sat there speechless watching him. He opened up the book and took a pen from his inside coat pocket. Then he began to write.

"You'll have to forgive me. I've never been real good with all the legal parts. So, let's set some guidelines. When said wishes are granted, Wisher, that's you, cannot present a wish that will: One, interfere with another person's free will."

He paused and smiled at the two of us.

"Two, bring someone back to life. Ah yes, that is vital isn't it?"

Again he looked both of us in the eyes. I had to look away.

"And three—this one is important—said wish cannot be something Wisher has the power to acquire on his or her own. Yes, I like that one."

He paused again and then went on.

"So, there you have it. Oh, yes, and let's put a time limit on it. Say, thirty days."

He then closed the book and put the pen back in his coat pocket. I was confused by the rules.

"It can be anything?" I asked.

Charles held up his index finger as if to caution me.

"Within the rules," he said.

Lisa and I both just looked at him in amazement. Then he looked at me and spoke again.

"On a personal note, it is my belief that this experience will bring your heartbeat back."

"My heartbeat?"

"Yes, listen closely."

He reached over to Lisa and me and put a hand on each of our shoulders. He closed his eyes and took a deep breath.

"Listen." We looked at each other and then back at him. He still had his eyes closed with his head tilted back.

"Do you hear it?" he asked.

"No," we both responded.

"Listen closer," he urged.

Then all of a sudden I could hear a faint heartbeat. It seemed to be coming from behind Lisa. She could hear, too, and was looking around to see where it had come from.

Charles smiled and then said, "Do you hear how fast it is? That's because it is a woman's heartbeat—always a little faster than a man's. Not many people know that."

Then he opened his eyes and took his hands off of our shoulders. The sound of the heartbeat faded away.

"Stanley, I bet you haven't heard your heartbeat in a while, have you?"

"No," I replied.

"You will hear it when your life is in rhythm and there is no doubt that you are doing what you were made to do. That's your heartbeat. That's when you're truly alive and not just existing. I want you to get your heartbeat back. You can, if you are willing to believe you can."

He paused for a moment and gave me a big smile. All I could do was stare into his deep brown eyes. Then he spoke again.

"So…I guess I'll see you in thirty days. And remember, all things are possible if you just believe they are."

He stood up and grabbed his hat and cane off the counter. I then noticed that the journal was not on the table and his reading glasses were gone. Where did they go? Lisa and I just sat there mesmerized by him. He seemed to get uncomfortable for a moment.

"Yes, this part is always awkward, isn't it?"

He reached out his arm and pointed at the doorway to the dining room.

"Hey, what's that?"

When we turned our heads to look, we heard the same swoosh noise as when Charles first appeared. When we looked back to see where he was standing, he was gone. I looked at Lisa and she at me. I looked down and saw the lamp on the counter. I picked it up and pushed it away from me.

This changed everything.

Chapter Seven

Just Believe

"Our life is what our thoughts make it. A man will find that as he alters his thoughts toward things and other people, things and other people will alter towards him."

James Allen

That night I sat in front of my computer, staring at it. Something was different now. I had a sense that there might be an answer to my problems on the horizon.

The words Charles had said rang through my head. There were two in particular: *JUST BELIEVE.*

I opened up a new document on my computer and typed those two words. All of a sudden, I was writing again. When I wrote those two words down, ideas started to flood my mind. I spent the next several hours typing my ideas into this document. Something had changed in me. For the first time in two years, I had a sense of hope. All because of a strange old man and two simple words.

Just Believe

That night I dreamed the same dream again—the one where I lose Eddy. It is the same every time; I wake up feeling a sense of total despair.

This morning was different though. When I awoke, I still had the sense of loss and loneliness, but the heavy feeling of depression wasn't as strong. I looked at the clock. It read 6:15 A.M.

If I get up now, I thought, *I will be up before Lisa.* That would be a first in a mighty long time.

I got up and walked softly down the hallway across our wood floors. It didn't matter how softly you walked, the floors still creaked with every step.

I stopped in the doorway to our room. Cooper was lying on the floor next to the bed, as he had done every night since the accident. I think he had taken on the role as caregiver to Lisa.

Lisa was sleeping in our bed. She looked like a little angel all cuddled up in her blankets. My side of the bed was smooth and neat, as it had been for the previous two years.

As I stood there for a moment watching her, it made me think of Eddy when he was a toddler. When he got old enough to sleep in a bed, he would wake up every morning around 6 A.M. and try to sneak into our bed. We could hear him coming down the hall. The floor creaked with every little step. That, and the squishing of his diaper, would always give him away. We would lay there pretending to be asleep, and he would try to climb up our bed. When he would get about halfway up, I would jump up at him and growl. He would squeal with delight, and

86

then he would cuddle in between us and start telling us stories of what we were going to do that day.

As I watched her lying there, I was sad more for her than anything else. Not only had she lost a son, she lost her husband, too.

Normally when I got out of bed, Lisa would be gone, and I would just hide from the day. Today was different. I had a sense of energy that I had not felt in a long time. How could this be? What was different? All that happened was a simple conversation with a strange old man. Two words. Those two words kept ringing through my head: *just believe.*

I grabbed a quick cup of coffee and headed out to the garage. I wanted to get a jump-start on it before I changed my mind.

About an hour and half had passed, and I was making progress. I was going through the piles of boxes and trying to determine what was in each of them. I created piles to keep and throw away. As I was piling some boxes in the driveway, I noticed Lisa watching me from the kitchen window. I didn't want to acknowledge her because she would make a big deal of it. So I just kept working.

A couple of moments later Cooper came running out to greet me. Then Lisa was off to work in the SUV. She didn't say anything to me as she left. I was actually glad. I didn't want her to make a big deal out of me cleaning the garage. Maybe she knew that it would embarrass me.

I worked on the garage for a couple of hours. The neighbor kids had been playing in their backyard. Our yards were connected, so sometimes they would work their way into my backyard. I had told them before to stay off my land, but they didn't seem to care.

The older boy and the older girl were playing catch. They were making a lot of noise, and it was really beginning to irritate me. All of a sudden, a baseball came out of nowhere and flew into the garage. It hit a jar of nails that fell on the floor and scattered all over the ground.

That's IT! I thought to myself.

I grabbed the ball and came around the corner.

"Why don't you brats learn how to throw!" is all I could think to say.

I have to hand it to the girl, the one they call Josh. I don't think that is her actual name, I think it is short for something. She was very much a tomboy and the name seemed to fit her. She stood her ground and didn't move. The older boy and the kid in the wheelchair took off as fast as they could. I threw the ball back at her hard. Probably harder than I should have, but I wanted to prove a point. She snapped up and caught it.

"I know how to throw," she said with all the bravery she could muster.

"No, you don't," I said as I turned and walked back into the garage to clean up the mess.

The next thing I know, this Josh kid is standing right next to me in the garage, as if she were challenging me. Two steps behind her was the younger girl. She had a stuffed bunny in her arms that looked like it had been burned in a fire. This one creeped me out a bit. She never talked. She just stood there and looked at me as if she were looking right through me.

Josh didn't waste any time. "My coach says I have a great arm!"

"Well, then your coach is an idiot," I replied.

"Yeah? Well, whadda you know?!" she challenged.

"Apparently, more than your coach," I countered.

I could tell that one really got to her. "Yeah, well at least I'm not the crazy dog guy!"

"What is that supposed to mean?"

"I've seen you at our practices talking to your dog."

I didn't know what to say to that. I think she could tell she got to me. I looked up at her from the floor where I was still scooping up nails, and then over to the quiet kid. By this time, Cooper had worked his way over to her, and she was petting him. Josh jumped back in on me.

"Whadda you doing watching us play all the time?" she quizzed.

"None of your business, kid. Go away! Cooper, come here now!" I grabbed the can of nails and stood up to take them to the workbench. This conversation was over as far as I was concerned. Josh was worked up and didn't like the fact that I walked away from her.

"Come on, Rachael. Let's go."

Josh took off back to her house. I was standing at the bench trying to look busy until they left. The quiet one who I now knew was named Rachael walked into the garage behind me. I didn't want to turn around to see what she was up to, so I just started straightening things up on the workbench.

Just Believe

I could hear her behind me. She picked something up off the floor and was coming toward me. I looked over my left shoulder, and I could see that she had picked up a nail that I had missed on the floor. She walked over to me slowly and put the nail on the bench. She looked up at me for a moment and then walked away.

I am not sure why that affected me, but it did. This kid who apparently had some issues was nice to me, and I was being such a jerk. What was my problem? Why did I have to take my anger out on these kids? I had to do something to make it right. So I did what came naturally to me with kids. I became Coach Walters.

I stepped out of the garage and saw the two of them walking across my yard toward their house.

I belted out, "You sling it too much."

Josh stopped dead in her tracks. "Excuse me?"

"Your arm. You have strength, but no form," I called out to her.

"I throw better than everybody else on my team," she replied.

"That may be true, but you don't throw as well as you could," I countered. I pointed to the back of my yard along the wooden fence. "Go over there and throw me the ball."

I could tell she didn't know what to expect. I am sure she wondered why I was nice to her all of a sudden. For me, it was a way to alleviate my guilt.

Josh walked over along the fence about 25 feet from me. Rachael sat on the ground behind me. Cooper, of course, made his way to her. He was always a sucker for a good petting session.

"OK. Throw me the ball," I instructed Josh.

She tossed the ball to me as if she were throwing the ball sidearm.

"You see. Right there: You throw from your side."

"No, I don't," she protested.

"Yes, you do. It's…well, you throw like a girl. Just a bit."

She raised one eyebrow at me and gave me a look that I have seen from several other women in my life. I think they must all be born with these looks.

"You gotta bring your arm back more, then up, over, and through," I said as I demonstrated for her. "You are using too much of your arm."

"What else would I use?" she asked.

"You need to use more of your body, or you'll just wear your arm out," I explained further.

She just looked at me as if I were speaking a foreign language to her. I took the ball and demonstrated again.

"Look here. If you shift your weight to your left leg a little sooner, you'll get more power in your throw." I tossed the ball back to her. "Try it like I showed you."

She went through the motions a couple of times, bringing her arm up over her body.

"Yes! Like that. Now concentrate and throw it to me."

She whipped the ball right at me. I caught it with my bare hands, and it stung.

"Ow!! Dang it!"

Just Believe

I dropped the ball on the ground. Josh was surprised by how hard she threw the ball. I picked the ball up.

"Don't you have a glove, mister?" she asked me.

It was a simple question, but of course it upset me. The last time I had my glove on, I was playing catch with Eddy. He had his new birthday glove. As a matter of fact, we were playing catch in this very same spot. I could feel the anger growing inside of me.

"No. No, I don't. Not anymore."

I had to get out of there before I did or said something terrible to this kid. I tossed the ball back to her and just walked away. She watched me for a moment with a look of total confusion on her face and then she started practicing the arm movement I had just taught her. I wasn't too proud of myself for letting the anger get the best of me, but at least I didn't yell at her.

I went back to work in the garage to keep my mind occupied. I reached up to one of the boxes on the top of the pile and took it down. As I was carrying it to the front of the garage, the bottom fell out, spreading all of its contents over the floor with a loud crash.

"Great, just great!" I blurted out.

I bent down to start picking up the contents when Josh came running over to me.

"Are you okay?" she asked.

Here we go again. I had just tried to get away from this kid, and she came right back to me. Maybe if I ignore her she will go away. I didn't give her an answer, but that didn't deter her.

"So…where did you learn so much about baseball?" she asked.

I stopped what I was doing for a second and looked up at her.

"What?"

"I mean did you play when you were a kid or—"

I had to cut her off. I didn't want to get into a conversation about my history.

"Listen, kid. I don't have time for all your questions, so unless you wanna pitch in and help clean up this mess then just leave me alone. OK?"

She just stood there looking at me.

"Yeah, that's what I thought."

I finished putting the last of the items back in the box and then stood up to put the box on the workbench.

Josh just stood there looking at me. Rachael was now sitting on the steps going into the house, and of course Cooper was sitting there being petted. From the backyard, I could hear Miss Esther yelling for Josh. Josh continued to stand there looking at me. I was starting to feel bad about the way I talked to her. Miss Esther walked up to the front of the garage.

"Josh, what are you doing here?" Josh didn't answer right away. I turned to look at her.

"I'm helping Mr. Walters straighten up his garage," she replied.

I turned around and gave Josh a curious look. Miss Esther was just as surprised by the answer as I was.

"Is that true, Mr. Walters?" Miss Esther inquired.

" I…well, uh…" I stammered.

Josh looked at me and said, "You did say I could stay if I helped you clean up this mess."

She had me.

"Yes, I did say that, but…."

Josh smiled and looked over to Miss Esther. "You see, I'm helping Mr. Walters."

Miss Esther knew something was up, but she didn't know how to respond. To be honest, I didn't know how to respond either. I had been a total jerk to this kid, but she still wanted to hang out with me. I didn't get it. Miss Esther broke the silence.

"OK then. Don't stay too long. You've got practice this afternoon," Miss Esther reminded her.

"OK," replied Josh.

Miss Esther got a look on her face as if she knew what Josh was up to. I wished she would let me in on the secret.

"Well, since it looks like I'm stuck with you, help me put the rest of this stuff back in this box," I said.

We went to work and didn't say anything for the next few minutes.

A couple of hours later, the midday sun was high in the sky. I had gotten the girls some glasses of lemonade, and we had just finished our break. Josh had proven to be a big help. We had gone through several boxes and were now working stacking and tying piles of newspapers.

"When you're done with that, we can haul them to the end of the driveway," I told her.

"I haven't worked this hard since I stayed with the farmer," she replied.

"How long have you been in foster care?" I asked.

"About three years. This is my fourth home."

"Really? Four foster homes in three years?" I was amazed.

"Yeah, they tell me I have some anger issues." She looked away, a little embarrassed. Little did she know I totally understood where she was coming from.

"Really?"

"I'm not looking for fights. But it's just not right for someone big to hurt someone small, especially moms or kids. People like that should be punished for what they do," she said angrily.

I could see the pain in her eyes as she said this. I felt sorry for her.

"I promised Miss Esther that I wouldn't fight anymore. She wants me to stay with her until DHS finds me a family."

"Do you like living with Miss Esther?" I asked.

"Yeah, she is great. But the real reason I am here is to take care of Rachael."

Josh looked over at Rachael, who was sitting on a cooler in the driveway. Cooper was at her side. She just stared off as if she were on another planet.

"What is her story?" I asked.

"I don't know what happened. Everyone talks about *the accident* and that she hasn't talked since. I understand her though, and she understands me. We don't need words to communicate."

I just looked at Rachael and wondered what could have happened to her to make her stop talking. Maybe the burnt stuffed bunny had something to do with it.

Just Believe

I could tell that Josh felt the conversation was getting a little too serious, so she tried to change the subject.

"So, what else do you do, besides take forever to clean your garage?"

"Oh, um, well, actually I'm a writer. I write books," I explained.

It felt almost strange to say that since I had not written anything in a long time. On the other hand, it was nice to say that. I was a writer. I needed to write.

"Wow. You must be rich," said Josh admiringly.

I had to laugh. "Hah…not exactly."

Josh went back to work on the papers, and I started to sort some of my tools on the bench.

Then she said, "I wish I had a lot of money."

That caught my attention. The word *wish*. Charles had said I could have three wishes, and now this kid said she wished she had a lot of money. It caught me by surprise.

"What did you just say?" I asked.

"I just said that I wish I had a lot of money," she said.

"What would you do with it, if your wish came true?" I inquired.

"Oh, I could do all kinds of things, like buy Miss Esther a much bigger house, or get new uniforms for my baseball team, or, I dunno, maybe finally get a family that would adopt Rachael and me. If I had money, someone would want to adopt us."

Could money be the thing that could turn this little girl's life around? Could money take care of my problems? I knew it couldn't bring my child back to me. I must have drifted off in my train of thought. Josh watched for a few moments, and then I think she was afraid I was going to get weird again.

"Well…I think we better be going. Come on, Rachael."

She got up quickly and snapped me out of my trance. They were halfway across the yard before I reacted. I scrambled out of the garage.

"Wait! Josh," I exclaimed.

They both stopped and turned around to me. I had stopped them, now I needed to say something, but what do I say? I wanted to say, *I'm sorry I was such a jerk*, or *I am sorry that your parents didn't love you enough to keep you*. But all that came out was, "Here's five dollars, for the work." I handed her a five-dollar bill.

"You don't need to pay me," she replied.

"Well…who said it was for you? It's to help your team…for the uniforms."

She smiled at me and took the money. "Thanks, but we're going to need a lot more than this."

I laughed. "Well, this garage ain't gonna clean itself. I could use your help if you're up to it."

She smiled and turned around and started walking back to her house. "I'll see you tomorrow, Mr. Walters."

"Bye," I said as I watched them walk away. I actually smiled. It was nice.

That night I got an idea. I went into my office and typed: *MONEY. Is money the most important thing in life? Can you be happy without it, or does it bring happiness? Will money solve all of my problems?*

Just Believe

I guess I had never thought of this before my conversation with Josh. She thought that money would solve all of her problems, and yet if she had a lot of money, would that bring her parents back? Would it bring her true love in her life?

I think many people believe that all of their problems would go away if they had a lot of money. I have known a lot of people in my life, and some of them have been very wealthy. The wealthiest were not always the happiest people on the earth. Most of them were consumed with how much money they had and how they were going to get more. They had built their identity on their status with money, and in the end, they had become pretty shallow. Mind you, I am not saying this is true for everyone who has a lot of money. There are those that have an understanding that money is a tool to be used to change the world.

I have heard it said, "The most fun you will have with money is when you give it away." It's true. Being able to give to a good cause or being able to help out a friend or neighbor is fun. It is rewarding. It is satisfying.

On the opposite side, having money does not bring with it any guaranteed happiness. There are many who do not have a lot of money and yet they are very happy people. You never meet someone who has experienced a lot of life and in the end would take money or positions over people.

I remember a guy we met on vacation one time who was 70 years old. He and his wife were camping next to us at a campground. We got to talking one night, and he was telling me about his life and family.

He said, "My daughter is a very successful lawyer up in Atlanta. She has her own family now, but we don't get to see much of her. It's kind of funny, because she has a beach house in Florida and a house in the mountains in Steamboat Springs, Colorado, but she hardly ever uses them. Heck, we use them more than she does."

He paused for a second and then went on. "I wish she would realize that the money or the positions are only temporary. It's the people in your life that matter. She makes lots of money and has a large firm, but she hardly knows her kids. She says she is doing it for them, and she wants them to have the things that she didn't have when she was growing up.

"I think her heart is in the right place, but her methods are a little off. She is ignoring the very thing that really makes her rich: her family. I wish she could see that the only thing worth having at the end of your life is the love of family and friends, not the houses or the stuff that goes with it. It is the people who you love and who love you back."

I never forgot that man. What he said left a great impact on me. That was when Eddy was about seven years old. He loved to go camping. I would give any amount of money to have him back.

Coming back to the wishes. Would I wish for money? Yes. Not because I thought it was going to make me happy, but because I needed to pay some bills. If this

Charles guy wanted to give me money, then I would gladly take it.

While I was sitting at my desk writing, Lisa came home from work. She stopped in the doorway of my office and watched me type for a moment. I pretended not to notice her. I just kept typing away hoping she would keep moving. I was not ready to try to explain what was happening with me. How would I explain that I might actually believe what this Charles guy was saying? Heck, I didn't understand it myself. But again those words seemed to haunt me: just believe. Is that the key? Can believing be enough? I didn't know just yet, and I certainly didn't want to try to explain it to her. So I just kept typing until she walked away.

That night I dreamed of Eddy again. It was the same dream that ended the same way. I can still hear his voice. "Let me go, Dad!" His last words still haunt me.

I awoke with a jolt. I had sweat on my forehead. I looked up at the clock: 5:23 A.M. I figured that I might as well get up. I didn't want to go back to sleep and dream again.

I got up and made some coffee and headed out to the garage. It was garbage day, so I started piling boxes and newspapers up at the end of the driveway. Lisa was watching me from the window again. I don't think we had talked since Charles had shown up. I really didn't know what to say to her. When I looked at her, I was reminded of how badly I had treated her. So I just didn't look at her.

She left the house to go to work at about 7:30 A.M. She must have had some early clients. She waved as she left. I just waved back and went into the garage.

I had cleared out about half of the garage and had about a dozen boxes in the driveway. I was now getting into all of the personal items that we had stowed away over the years. Josh and Rachael came walking over.

"Hey, Mr. Stan," called out Josh.

Huh, *Mr. Stan*. We had graduated from Mr. Walters. Josh was a pretty straightforward kid. I kind of liked that about her. That is probably how she had survived her life so far. Rachael, with the burnt bunny under her arm, found her spot on her favorite seat, the old cooler, and sat down to watch us work. I looked at Josh.

"I wasn't sure you were going to show," I said.

"You said you needed help," she responded.

"Yeah, I just didn't think you were serious," I admitted. We both walked back into the garage to a large pile of boxes.

"So, what are we doing today?" she asked.

"Well, we need to go through all of these boxes and see what's in them. Then we'll decide what to get rid of and what to keep."

"OK," she replied.

I handed her a box to put in the throwaway pile. "Take this one and put it on that pile."

She complied and took the box out into the driveway. I noticed Cooper made a beeline for Rachael as soon as she sat down, hoping for a nice petting session. Then he got up and walked way back deep into the garage. I wasn't sure where he was going.

There was a small hole in the pile of stuff that he crawled into. When he came back out, he had his old beat-up tennis ball that he and Eddy used to play with. I was amazed that he knew where it was. By this time, Josh had returned and was watching me watch him. She seemed a bit confused by it all.

"Would you look at that," I said.

"What?" Josh asked.

"The ball. He hasn't brought that out in…years." We both watched for a moment as Cooper made his way out of the garage and over to Rachael sitting on the cooler in the driveway. When he got to her, he set the ball on the ground at her feet. Rachael took notice and leaned down to pick it up. As she did, she set the stuffed bunny on the ground.

"Wow!" Josh said.

"What?" I asked.

"Rachael…she has never let go of that bunny. Miss Esther even has to put it in a plastic bag when she takes a bath," Josh explained.

"Really?" I said as we both watched in amazement.

Rachael took the ball and threw it for Cooper. Cooper quickly sprung into action and went after the ball. He loved to play fetch. He quickly brought the ball back to her and she threw it again. Once again, Cooper took off after the ball. I think I actually saw a slight smile on Rachael's face. It was fascinating.

I whispered. "Way to go, Coop."

Josh looked up at me and smiled.

"Well, let's get back to work here," I said in my mock-boss voice. "Enough dilly-dallying."

Josh laughed as I handed her another box.

We went through about a dozen boxes over the next hour. We found items that I had forgotten we owned. I even found stuff that I had kept from high school. It was time for a lot of this stuff to go.

I was working on a box of tools as Josh was going through a box of pictures. I could hear her laughing, so I looked over the pile of boxes to see what was going on.

"What are you laughing at?" I asked.

"This picture," she pointed at an old photo.

Of course, she found a high school picture of me wearing wide lapels and sporting a mullet.

"Hey, you hush up!" I said playfully. "That was the style in those days. Business in front and party in the back."

Josh couldn't contain herself and let out a hearty laugh. I started to laugh, too. It felt good.

"So, is this in the keep pile or the throwaway pile?" she asked.

"Unfortunately, keep."

I went back to work on my box and Josh came over and sat on a box next to me.

"Mr. Stan?"

"Yes," I replied.

"I was thinking…about what we talked about yesterday. I want to change my wish."

"Really? OK, what would you like to change it to?" I asked her.

"I was thinking about what is really important in life. I would wish for a family...like you and Mrs. Stan have."

That statement came out of left field. A family like me and Lisa. I wasn't even sure if we were a family. I didn't know what to say.

I just said, "Like *what*?"

"Like you have. I mean look at all you have. You have a beautiful house, a great dog, nice neighbors... You have everything anyone could want," Josh explained.

The kid was right. What was my problem? I did have a lot of great things in my life, but for some reason all I could see is what I didn't have. The kid had opened my eyes a little.

"I guess I haven't thought of it that way," I told her.

"Yeah. Your wife works so you can play all day. The way I see it, you've got it made."

I had to laugh. Only a kid would have this perspective on the situation. But then again, she did have a point.

We both went back to working on boxes. Josh finished with the box she had and opened up another. She started to dig around and then I could hear her talking to me.

"Aw man. A Rawlings QS435! This is awesome!"

What did she say? It took me a second to register what she just said. Rawlings QS435. The words rang in my head for a second. That was Eddy's glove. The one I got him for his birthday. I looked over at her, and she was putting the glove on her hand. I looked down and saw the box. It had *Eddy's Things* written on the side. What was she doing in that box?

The next moment was a blur. I could feel my blood pressure rising, and I lurched at her before I had a chance to think about what I was doing.

"Put that away now!" I growled.

"Why? This is great. Can I use it?" she asked innocently.

"No! Give that to me now!" I grabbed the glove out of her hand, and it freaked her out. She went from a cute, fun little girl to a scared little rabbit. She cowered up against the wall of the garage as I unleashed my venom on her.

"You don't just take things that aren't yours," I yelled at her as I stuffed the glove back in the box and folded the flaps shut in a spasm of movement.

To my surprise she came right back at me.

"Oh yeah, well, you don't have to yell at me. That's not how you treat someone, ya know."

I turned around and placed the box high up on the top of a pile of boxes. I tried to control myself, but I just kept blurting out in anger.

"You just need to keep out of this box."

My back was completely turned to her now. She continued to yell back at me.

"You don't yell at people like that. And you don't hit people, either."

Where did that come from? I may be a jerk, but I would never hit her. I turned back around.

"What? Hit you? I didn't..." I said full of surprise.

By now she was crying. Her face was filled with rage. I knew there was a lot more to this little girl than was on the surface. I can only imagine what she had been through.

"I thought you were my friend. You don't treat your friends like that. Come on, Rachael. Let's go."

Josh and Rachael both walked out of the garage and down the driveway. Cooper got up for a moment, looked at me and then started following the two girls.

"Cooper, stay here," I called after him. He just kept walking. "COOPER! Come now!"

He stopped for a moment and looked back at me. He gave me a look as if to say, *You're a bad man*, and then he turned and caught up to the girls. I just watched them all walk away.

"Stupid dog!"

I sat in the garage for a while and then went into the house. I sat down at my computer and tried to write, but nothing came to me. I had crossed the line with this little girl, and I knew it. I couldn't hide from it anymore. I had to stop hurting people. I had to do as Charles had said. I needed to let go of the pain. It was killing me, and only hurting all those around me, but how could I let it go? How would I make this change in my life? I had lived with this pain for two years, and it had become a way of life for me.

Charles' words kept coming back to me. I had embraced the lie and now my whole life was wrapped around it. I needed to do something to make it right with Josh. I needed to stop being so selfish and think of her. I needed to make a personal sacrifice. What could I do for her that would show her that I was truly sorry?

The glove.

I got the glove out of the garage and headed over to Miss Esther's house. I would ask her to forgive me and give her the glove. This would show her that I was truly sorry.

I walked up the wooden stairs to the porch on the backside of her house. I stood there for a second. I was breathing hard and my skin was flushed. I thought to myself, *Calm down. It's just a little girl.* But I knew it was much more than that. For me, it was a step on my way out of this grave that I had buried myself in.

After a couple of moments and some breathing exercises, I knocked on the door. The oldest boy came to the door. I thought his name was Austin. When he opened the door, he had a bowl of cereal in his hands and was munching on a mouthful.

"Hey, is Josh here?" I asked.

He looked at me for a moment and then turned, nodded his head, and walked away. I stood there for several moments until I heard someone coming down the hallway. It was Miss Esther. She didn't look too happy. She stepped out onto the porch, closed the door, and crossed her arms on her chest.

"Hello, Mr. Walters. May I help you?"

Wow, this woman was tough. She was not happy with me, and she was not afraid to show it.

"Hi Esther. Do you think I could speak with Josh?" I asked.

"I don't think it is a good idea for you to talk with her anymore," Miss Esther replied.

I was embarrassed. "I know. I *am* sorry. I lost my temper. If I could just talk to her, I could…." I trailed off.

"You have to understand Josh's past. She doesn't know how to process anger," Miss Esther explained.

"I know I crossed the line. If I could, I would really like to talk with her," I said sincerely.

"Well, she's not here now," she replied.

That was it. She shut me down.

"Oh, OK. I understand."

I slowly turned around and walked back down the stairs. I could feel her gaze on the back of my head. I had mixed feelings. For the first time in a long time, I was going to try to do something to help someone else, and I was shut down. I got to the bottom of the stairs and then I heard Miss Esther call my name.

"Mr. Walters, you know it's a nice day for a walk. Maybe you should take a walk down by the ball field."

She had a look of compassion on her face. I was totally surprised.

I snapped out of my daze and said, "Thanks, Esther."

I took a couple of steps down the driveway and she called after me. "Now, don't you go making a fool out of me."

I turned and smiled at her. "I won't. I promise."

As I walked down the road to the ball field, I stuffed the glove in the back of my pants. I was trying to figure out what I was going to say. What do you say to a little girl who you just crushed with your words? *I'm sorry* didn't seem like it was enough. This made me think of Lisa. I should be saying this to her as well. Was it too late for that? Would she believe me if I told her I was sorry? I really didn't know what to do.

When I rounded the corner, I saw the ball field. The team was all there practicing. Rachael was sitting in the stands behind home plate with Cooper by her side. As I walked past, she looked up at me and then looked away. Cooper looked up at me as well and then laid his head back down.

"Traitor," I said under my breath, though I understood why he was mad at me.

Josh was on the pitcher's mound throwing balls at a batter. She was using the technique I taught her, and the batter didn't stand a chance. She looked over at me in between pitches. I stood on the other side of the backstop, waiting for the right moment.

The coach sent her in to bat.

"You're up next. Go grab a bat!"

This was my opportunity.

She came in from the field headed to the dugout. I walked over to meet her.

"Hey, Josh, can I talk to you for a second?"

She kept moving as if I weren't there. She dropped her glove and picked out a batter's helmet and a bat.

"Make it quick. I need to get back to practice," she said with a harsh bitterness to her words.

I wish I had practiced what I was going to say better.

"Listen, Josh. I know what I did was wrong. I lost my temper, and there is no excuse for that."

She wouldn't look at me. She stood there with her bat looking at the ground.

The catcher chimed in. "Come on, Josh, you're up."

Josh turned and started walking to home plate.

"I gotta go," she said.

Now I was desperate.

"Josh, wait. Please." She stopped and looked at me impatiently. "This is really important. Please let me finish."

She took two steps toward me and I knew I didn't have much time, so I went for it.

"OK, I'll cut to the chase. I lost my temper and I was wrong. Can you please forgive me?"

She looked up at me for a moment that felt like hours. Then she walked up to the fence and looked me straight in the eyes.

"What?" I asked her as she stared at me.

"I just need to see into your eyes," she replied.

"My eyes? Why?" I was puzzled.

"To make sure you're not lying," she said matter-of-factly.

I bent over so we were eye to eye through the fence. She moved in closer until we were only about ten inches apart. She stared into my eyes, and I looked straight back at her. I wanted her to know I was serious. After about a minute, I needed to know.

"Well?" I asked.

"You're doing alright," she replied. I think that was her way of saying she forgave me.

"Good," I said as I reached around behind me and pulled the glove out of my back pocket. "Cause I wouldn't have been able to give you this."

She squealed with delight. "For real?" she asked.

She ran around to me through an opening in the fence about 10 feet away. She grabbed the glove, squealed again, and then ran back to her teammates who had all congregated around the pitcher's mound watching our exchange. I looked up to see all of them, and I was a little embarrassed. The coach gave me a big smile and a thumbs-up.

Josh got to the team and then stopped. I had walked over to the opening in the fence and was standing there. I think I was smiling. All I know is that I was happy. She turned around, looked at me for a moment, and then started walking back to me. She was smiling from ear to ear. When she reached me, she took her finger and gave me the *come here* sign to bend over. When I did, she leaned in and kissed me on the cheek.

"Thank you, Mr. Stan," is all she said.

She looked at me with big, beautiful, blue eyes full of forgiveness, and then turned and ran back to the team. I was frozen in time. I stayed bent over for a moment. I could feel the blood coursing through my veins. My heart was pounding so hard in my chest I was sure that my shirt was moving.

As I slowly started to stand back up, I could hear the faint sound of a heartbeat. It seemed so surreal, almost like this had all been a scene in a movie. The sound got louder and louder until all other sounds seemed to disappear, and the heartbeat was all I could hear.

Then Charles' voice echoed in my mind.

"You will hear your heartbeat again when your life is in rhythm, and there is no doubt that you're doing what you were made to do. That's your heartbeat; that's when you're truly alive and not just existing"

I took a long, slow breath in and savored the moment. I looked down and noticed that I had put my hand on my chest.

Just then Sam walked up behind me and whispered in my ear. "It does a heart good to help heal another person." Then he walked away as silently as he had appeared.

More than you know, Sam. More than you know, I thought to myself.

Chapter Eight

The Power of the Message

*"Faith is taking the first step even when you
don't see the whole staircase."*
Martin Luther King, Jr.

I could hear my heartbeat. I had not heard it in two years. Life was different now. As I walked back home, I was thinking about what had just happened. I was amazed to realize that the very thing that I was so mad at Lisa about was the thing that set me free. Lisa had taken Eddy's clothes to the garage sale, and I was so mad I was willing to throw away everything including our marriage. But, when I was willing to give Eddy's glove to Josh, I found forgiveness in the eyes of a child. It amazes me how life can be so ironic.

I knew I had to do something to make it up to Lisa. I needed to ask her to forgive me. To be honest, I was scared at the thought. I did not deserve to be forgiven. I had done nothing but hurt her over the past two years, and now all of a sudden I was going to ask her to forgive me. Then those two words appeared in my head: *just believe.* I had to do it, and I was going to do it the only way I knew how: Make her dinner.

I spent the rest of the afternoon cleaning up the house. Lisa has always been a good housekeeper, but I think she was worn out by the stress of dealing with me. I washed, vacuumed, dusted, and swept all of the rooms. I straightened out the furniture and all of the bookshelves. I wanted to create a safe atmosphere for her. I wanted her to see that I had put some effort into this.

I was in the kitchen when Lisa came home. She walked through the living room and noticed how clean and neat it was. Then she came into the dining room and saw the table. The room was lit with candles. I had set the table with fresh flowers, about six candles, bread, and of course the lamp was in the center. She stopped and stood there for a couple of minutes, not sure what to think. Then she saw me in the kitchen stirring a pot of sauce. She stepped into the room and stood in the doorway. She was still dressed in her gym clothes.

She got my attention with a little clearing of her throat, "Ah-hum."

"Oh, hey. I didn't hear you come in. Um, dinner will be ready in a minute. Why don't you go get changed," I suggested to her.

She stood in the doorway looking at me as if she couldn't believe what she was hearing.

"Go on, change. Diner will be ready in a few minutes."

She gave me a slight smile and then turned slowly without saying a word and walked away.

The Power of the Message

I filled up two plates with spaghetti and poured some sauce on top. I cut up some bread and put a little butter with garlic salt on top, just like I knew she liked it. I carried the plates out and set them on the table. Lisa walked in with a look of bewilderment still on her face. I could tell she did not know what to expect. The last time we had talked, I had told her I was leaving. Now I was making her dinner. I only hoped that she would listen to me and let me tell her what was happening to me.

I pulled a chair out for her to sit.

As she sat, she said. "Stanley, I don't know what to say here. This is amazing."

I could tell she was a little nervous and I didn't want to put the burden of conversation on her, so I quickly sat and then looked her in the eyes.

"Lisa, listen. Before you say anything, I have something I have to say to you."

Her eyes were focused on me. She wanted to hear what I had to say.

I continued. "This whole thing with Charles, and believing that things can be different...it has got me thinking. Then there's Josh."

"Josh? From next door?" Lisa asked, puzzled.

"Yeah, I hired her to help me clean the garage."

She gave me a look of surprise. I am sure she didn't know that I knew there was a kid living next door, let alone that I would know her name.

"Well, we were cleaning the garage and we were talking. She said something that took me by surprise."

I stopped for a second trying to figure out how to formulate my words.

"She said if she could have anything she wanted in life, it would be to have a happy family…just like you and me."

I could tell that cut her to the heart. Lisa looked away from me for a moment. I didn't say anything. I wanted to give her as much time as she needed.

"Are we a family, Stanley?" she asked quietly.

"Lisa, I really want us to be," I said.

She had to look away again, and I could see a tear forming in her eye. She swallowed hard and slowly looked back up at me.

"Stanley, I really want to believe you, but…"

She couldn't finish the sentence. I jumped in before I lost her. "Listen, something incredible happened today. I gave Eddy's baseball glove to Josh." I could tell that statement surprised her. She knew how important that glove was to me.

"You did?"

"It was something I knew I needed to do. When I did, you're never going to believe this…I actually heard the sound of my heartbeat. I know it sounds strange, but I could actually hear it," I explained.

This statement moved Lisa. Her eyes were wet with tears. My eyes were tearing up as well. I had to get it all out.

"Honey, you were right. For the last two years the thing I feared the most was letting go, as if doing so was wrong. But when I gave Josh that glove, I felt a sense of peace come over me. I haven't felt that in a long time, and now I feel like everything is different, like everything is going to be alright. Lisa, I'm so sorry for the way that I have treated you. Can you forgive me?"

She now had tears rolling down her cheeks. She reached over and put her hand on mine.

"Stanley, I forgive you, and I love you."

Then she leaned over and kissed me softly and tenderly. I could feel the love move through her body into mine. For the first time in two years, I was able to accept love again.

Chapter Nine

There Is No Magic

"A man sooner or later discovers that he is the
master-gardener of his soul, the director of his life."
James Allen

I was a new man. Over the next few weeks I was a writing machine. I started writing my story, which eventually became this book. My publisher loved the idea and gave me a huge advance. He said it was some of the best fiction he had seen in a long time. I tried to convince him that it wasn't fiction, that all of this had really happened to me. He just smiled and shook my hand. I guess it doesn't matter to me if he believed me or not. I know for myself these events were true and my life was changed as a result of the message.

I started getting up in the mornings and taking Cooper for walks. I was getting myself back in good physical shape. I moved back into the bedroom with Lisa. Now both sides of the bed are messy.

I went to the coach of the baseball team and volunteered my services. He gratefully accepted and made me head coach. He was so excited; he gave me his personal whistle right there on the spot. He stayed on as assistant and was a huge help. We were able to build a good team and actually started winning games.

Josh and Rachael came around more and more and continued to help me clean the garage. We got it pretty much cleaned out and organized. As a matter of fact, Josh and Rachael became regular guests at our dinner table. I think they spent more time at our house than at Miss Esther's. Life was good. We started taking them on outings to the park and the zoo and lots of other places. We really enjoyed our time with them. Life was good and only seemed like it was going to get better.

One Friday morning, I got up and was getting ready to take Cooper for his morning walk. I stopped by my office and noticed the calendar. It was the twenty-ninth day since we had met Charles. He was coming back tomorrow. I went in the kitchen where Lisa was pouring a cup of coffee.

"Did you realize that tomorrow is thirty days?" I mentioned.

"Really, I can't believe it has gone so fast. Are we ready?" she asked.

"I don't know. I'm not sure what it is we need to do to be ready. Everything is so different now," I replied.

She just nodded her head in agreement with me. I gave her a kiss and then headed out the door with Cooper.

The next day was Saturday, a Saturday much like any other. But this Saturday was going to be different. Charles was coming back. I could hardly sleep, but this time it wasn't because of a bad dream. Those had stopped altogether. This time it was because I was excited to see Charles and tell him of all that had happened.

Lisa and I were sitting in the living room on the couch. She had the lamp in her hands, and we were just waiting. I broke the silence.

"So, what are we supposed to do?" I asked.

"I don't know," she responded.

"I could go get the hammer," I joked.

She smiled and then read the side of the lamp. "Hmmm, *just believe*. I think I do."

Just then we heard a noise come from the kitchen that sounded like the toaster popping. We both got up and walked into the kitchen.

Standing by the toaster with two freshly toasted pieces of bread in his hands was Charles. He was humming to himself and spreading butter on the second piece of toast. Next to the plate was a freshly poured cup of coffee. He didn't hear us when we first stepped in. We stood in amazement and watched him for a few minutes. He picked up one of the pieces of toast and took a large bite out of it. He closed his eyes as we continued to watch him slowly chew his piece of toast. He then swallowed it and opened his eyes. As he did, he noticed us standing in the doorway watching him. We both let out a little chuckle, and he seemed to take it in stride.

"Ah, good morning," Charles said as he picked up his plate and cup of coffee and walked over to the center island and sat down. He placed the plate and cup of coffee in front of him and picked up a napkin and spread it out on his lap.

"I can't tell you how excited I am to hear about your wishes," he said.

He then took another bite of his toast and chased it down with a sip of the coffee. "Ahhhh. Now that's good."

We stood in front of him simply watching the show. We could tell he was enjoying himself, and we didn't want to stop him. After taking one more sip of coffee, he took his napkin and wiped the corners of his mouth and then his hands. Now he was ready to get down to business.

"Now then, let's hear those wishes. What have you got?"

I really did not know where to start. "Well, Charles, you see, we—Lisa and I—well, we, um…"

He looked at me trying to figure out what I was saying. *I* was trying to figure out what I was saying.

"Yes…" Charles encouraged me on.

Thankfully, Lisa jumped in to help me.

"I think what Stanley is trying to say is that we don't, well, we don't have any wishes."

Charles straightened up in his seat and got a playful smile on his face.

"You don't have any wishes? Well how can this be? If I remember correctly, you asked me for three wishes," he recollected.

I jumped back in. "Well, we had wishes, but they kind of got answered on their own," I explained.

Now he had a huge smile on his face. "Most fascinating. Do tell."

There Is No Magic

Lisa started out again. "Well, our first wish was to have lots of money. Well, that kinda happened."

"It happened?" Charles inquired.

He grabbed his notebook again and started thumbing through some pages. "I don't remember authorizing any wishes in regard to money."

I jumped back in. "No, no. It's not like that. It was because of the third wish."

"The third wish?" he asked.

I continued. "You see I wanted to do something I loved... so that was going to be my third wish. Then I got this idea for a book. Yeah, it just came to me. You will love the title."

I looked over at Lisa and she smiled and said *"Just Believe."*

Those two words set Charles off. He let out a series of belly laughs that could be heard throughout the house.

Once he subsided, I continued. "Yeah, I pitched the idea to my publisher and he flipped over it. I got the largest advance for a book in this publisher's history. So, that took care of wish number one. And, well, wish number three."

Charles listened intently as I explained and then put his journal away.

Then he said "Go on... what about wish number two?"

This was a hard one for me. It took me a moment to get my thoughts in order. Lisa leaned into me, and I put my arm around her.

Just Believe

"Well, wish number two just kind of happened all on its own. It took a child to show me what I needed. My second wish was for a happy family."

"Let me guess. It was there all along...you just couldn't see it," said Charles.

"Exactly. It was there all the time. I just didn't believe it any more."

Charles looked at the two of us for a moment and then stood up. He moved forward so we were only about a foot apart. He had a look of a pleased father, and I knew he was going to tell me something I needed to hear.

"Stanley. Lisa. I am so happy to hear that you have grasped the essence of this message. You see, most people go through life not understanding that they have been given this amazing gift. Each one of us has the ability to create the life we want. We just need to believe we can. This is a truth that has been passed down through the ages, and now the two of you have taken hold of it."

He paused and smiled big at us. "Now the question is, what will you do with this truth? Keep it to yourselves, or share it with others?"

"Share it with others?" I asked.

"Yes, Stanley. Now that you know the truth, you need to share it with others."

He paused again and looked each of us in the eye.

"When the time is right, you will know what to do. Do you know how I know? Because I believe in you."

And then he was gone. Nothing but half of a piece of toast to prove he was ever there.

There Is No Magic

After that meeting, I had a chance to digest what he had told us. The amazing thing that I did not realize, or even think was possible, is that all that I could have wished for was already in my grasp. All I had to do was change the way that I saw things.

It reminded me of *The Wizard of Oz* movie. Dorothy, the Scarecrow, the Tin Man, and the Cowardly Lion were all on a quest to find what they thought would make them happy in life. They were so committed to finding it that they embarked on a journey down the Yellow Brick Road. They faced all kinds of adversity and trials on their quest, and in the end, when they had reached their final goal of meeting the Wizard in the Emerald City, they found out that they already possessed everything they were looking for. They just had to be willing to see it.

I felt very much like them. For my wishes, I was asking for money, family, and work. When I took my eyes off of my issues, and was willing to just believe, I was able to start writing. Writing is something I love to do. When I came up with the idea of this book, my publisher loved it and gave me a large advance on the book. This brought the money. Family is one of those things that you can appreciate or take for granted. My eyes were so much on myself that I did not see the wonderful woman who was my wife. When I removed the blinders of fear and selfishness from my eyes, I was able to see Lisa for who she really was. At the end of my Yellow Brick Road, I realized that everything I could ever wish for was already in my midst. All I had to do was *believe* it was.

Chapter Ten

A Curve in the Road

"Change is the law of life. And those who look only to the past or present are certain to miss the future."

John F. Kennedy

After our meeting with Charles, I needed to have some time alone to digest the events of the past 30 days. I went out to work on the garage when I heard a ruckus outside. I stepped out to the driveway. A group of kids were coming down Miss Esther's driveway. It looked like Josh, Rachael, Austin, and Cody, the kid in the wheelchair. Alex, a very tomboyish girl who was a friend of Josh's, was walking with them, too. She also happened to be the catcher on our ball team.

They were making a lot of noise as they came down the driveway. I could tell something was up by the look on Josh's face. I walked over to them to see what was going on. When I got there, I noticed Josh wouldn't look me in the eye. She was covered with dirt, and she had a scrape on her left arm.

"Josh, what happened to you?" I asked rather alarmed.

Alex was all too proud to jump in and give the play by play.

"She just kicked Ronny Martin's butt."

All the kids let out a hearty laugh. Josh looked down at that ground. I could tell she was embarrassed. She had promised Miss Esther she wouldn't fight any more. I reached out and pulled her chin up to look at me.

"What...what happened?" I asked.

Once again, Alex couldn't wait to jump in. "Well, Ronny called Cody a freak."

I looked over at Cody in his wheelchair. He looked up at me with a sad look on his face. Alex continued, "And Josh told him to shut up. And then Ronny said to make him. So...she did!"

All the kids except Josh let out another round of laughs. I looked over to Josh again. "You okay? Josh?"

She looked up at me and nodded her head. All of a sudden, Cody came alive. I think he felt vindicated by Alex's story.

"You should have seen her. She was like a cage fighter."

He stuck his arms out as if he was doing some ultimate cage fighting move.

Miss Esther must have heard the noise, because she peeked her head out of the back door and, seeing us, came down the back stairs. Cody must have known trouble was on the way.

"Uh-oh," he said.

I had to chuckle to myself.

Miss Esther took a good look at Josh and let out a big sigh. "Josh, what have you done?"

"He started it," she protested.

"Go in the house and get cleaned up," ordered Miss Esther.

Josh looked back up at me almost to say she was sorry for what happened. All of the other kids were suddenly silent. They knew this was not good. Miss Esther gave them all a look that only a mother can give.

"Alex, it's probably a good idea for you to go home now," she said.

"OK," she said as she walked slowly down the driveway. Miss Esther turned and walked back toward the house. I could tell she was upset.

"That poor girl," she said.

"What's the problem?" I asked.

"She is really having a hard time with all of this," said Miss Esther.

"All of what?" I asked.

"She is being adopted," Miss Esther explained.

Adopted? Where did that come from?

I guess I had forgotten that Josh was a foster kid. Miss Esther and the DHS desired that Josh be placed in a permanent home. In my typical fashion, I blurted out the first thing that came to my mind, "Adopted?"

Miss Esther stopped about halfway up the stairs to her house and turned to me.

"Yes, she's had several visits with a prospective family."

"She hasn't said a word to me," I explained.

"That doesn't surprise me. She doesn't want to go with them," she said.

"How soon is this going to happen?" I asked.

"I'm not sure. Could be any time now. Depends on how the visits go. You have to understand, DHS wants this to be a good fit for her. If you ask me, they are going to have a rough time with it. She has grown attached to you and Lisa," she added.

"Wow. I never expected that," I replied.

She leaned in close to me and took a glance down the driveway. We could both see Rachael throwing the ball for Cooper. Then Esther looked back to me and spoke in a soft voice. "What makes this more difficult is that they don't want to adopt Rachael."

"What? They have to! Those two need each other." I couldn't believe what I was hearing.

Miss Esther continued, "I think the thing she is most upset about is leaving you."

I stood there for a moment letting it all sink in. Had I grown that attached to this little girl that I cared that she would be gone? I should be happy for her. She wanted a family, and now there was a loving couple that wanted to give her a good life. Breaking Josh and Rachael up would be hard on her. Josh treated her like a real sister.

"I can't believe she is leaving," I said.

Miss Esther could tell this was hard on me. She nodded her head and put a hand on my shoulder to console me.

All the time that we had been talking, Rachael had been playing fetch with Cooper. What we didn't know is that she had thrown the ball a little too hard, and it bounced down the driveway, out into the street, around a parked car, and out of sight. Cooper followed the path of the ball around the parked car and out of Rachael's line of sight. She stood there for a few moments waiting for Cooper to come back with the ball, but he didn't. Then all of a sudden, Rachael could hear the sound of a truck coming around the corner and driving down the road straight for where Cooper would be. She started walking forward but could not see Cooper. The truck was gaining speed and coming closer to where Cooper would be.

She looked back to see where we were. From where she was standing, she could see us talking on the back steps, but we were in a deep conversation and had not noticed what was going on with her. She looked back to the truck and then to the street, hoping Cooper would be coming back, but she saw nothing. She then looked back at us, trying to form words, but nothing was coming out. She looked back at the truck again, which was now only about 100 feet from where she was, and then back to us again, all while still trying to form words. She struggled with it. She wanted to scream, but nothing was coming out. She knew she had to do something or Cooper would get hit. She could feel the words way deep down inside of her wanting to come out. It was building energy like a volcano getting ready to explode.

She opened her mouth and a high-pitched scream came out and then the word, *"COOPER!"*

It startled Miss Esther and me. At first we had no idea what it was. I looked over to see Rachael with a look of total terror on her face. She yelled again, *"COOPER!"* and then turned and started running down the driveway toward the street.

All of a sudden, I flashed back to Eddy riding his bike down the driveway. I took off running "Rachael, STOP!" I cried out.

Rachael was in full stride. She dropped the bunny on the ground and had reached the sidewalk. I was running as fast as I could. It was like I was moving in slow motion. I could hear Miss Esther screaming behind me. By this time, we both could see the truck coming down the road.

I yelled out again, but to my surprise I yelled, "Eddy, stop!"

I was gaining on her. She had reached the back of the parked car. Eddy flashed in front of me. Then I saw Rachael again. I was reliving the accident, and I couldn't let it happen again. I looked over and saw that the truck was not slowing down and was quickly approaching the front of the car. Rachael was about to clear the back of the car as I grabbed and pulled her back, and the truck whizzed by.

I fell backward onto the slope of the driveway and held her tightly in my arms. I started to cry.

"Eddy, I am so *sorry*. I am *so sorry*," I said as I rocked Rachael in my arms.

Rachael looked up at me and said, "It's OK, Mr. Stan. It's OK."

I felt as though a huge weight had lifted off of me. For the first time in two years, I realized Eddy's death was an accident. Many people, including Lisa, had tried to tell me that, but I now truly understood it.

Cooper came running back to us with the ball in his mouth, wagging his tail. He had no idea what had just happened. I wasn't sure how I felt about that dog. I guess I was just happy he was safe.

Chapter Eleven

The Big Game

"Baseball is a lot like life. It's a day-to-day existence, full of ups and downs. You make the most of your opportunities in baseball as you do in life."

Ernie Harwell

It was Sunday, the day our baseball team would play the big game. I had not seen Josh since the fight, and I wanted to talk with her. I wanted to tell her that she should give the adoptive parents a chance. It was not that I wanted her to be adopted; I had just convinced myself that it was the best thing for her. To be honest I hated the idea. I wanted her to stay with us. I was very conflicted with the whole thing.

The team didn't know that I had combined the money that the parents from the team had raised with some of my own money to purchase new uniforms for them. The uniforms were navy blue shirts with gold letters on the front that spelled out our team name: *Tigers*. They looked great, and I couldn't wait to give them to all the players. I was loading the uniforms and gear in the back of the SUV when Miss Esther came walking down the sidewalk to me.

"Hey Esther, take a look at these."

I held up a shirt so she could see it. It was the number seven shirt. That was Eddy's number. I had to smile.

Esther smiled, "Those are great."

I was very pleased with the uniforms, and it showed.

"This is it. Last game of the season. They are going to look great!"

Miss Esther took a good look at the shirt and then focused her attention on me.

"Stanley, I wanted to tell you something before you go."

"What is it?" I asked as I continued loading up.

"I just got a call from Bernice, Josh's case worker. The adopting couple is coming to the game today. Josh is going to spend the night with them after the game. Tomorrow they will meet at the DHS office for the official placement."

I looked down at the number seven shirt and thought for a moment. Then I looked back up at her.

"I'm not sure what to say..."

"You don't need to say anything, dear. I just thought you would want to know," she replied.

"Thanks. See you at the game?"

Miss Esther flashed me that big smile of hers. "Go Tigers!"

It was game time. The kids had worked hard to get there. We were up against the number one team in the league, and I actually thought we had a chance to beat them! The bleachers were full of family, friends, and neighborhood fans. There was a charge in the air and you could feel it. The adoptive couple was in the stands as well. Josh was warming up with Alex and saw them come in and sit down. They gave Josh a big smile and waved at her. She gave them a halfhearted wave and then looked over at me. It seemed as though she felt like she was cheating on me. I gave her a big nod, and she went back to throwing the ball with Alex. I looked over to Lisa, and she tried to give me an encouraging smile, but I knew she felt the same way that I did.

The game took off well. We were playing a good game, but the other team was just a little better. The score was 5 to 2 after the third inning. Josh was pitching OK, but I could tell she was distracted. She hadn't said much of anything to me, and I felt as though she was upset with me.

We had the field and Josh was throwing a couple pitches in to Alex. There was a pudgy, blond-haired kid with what looked to be a black eye in the batter's box. I was standing in the opening of the fence at our bench when Jason, my first baseman, walked up to me.

"Uh-oh," he said.

"What?" I asked.

"That's Ronny Martin," he said.

The name sounded familiar, but I wasn't sure who he was. I looked at Jason, wanting to have more information.

"He is the kid Josh beat up last week for picking on Cody."

Just Believe

Oh, *that* Ronny Martin. He did look like a bully. Ronny stepped up to the plate and took his position. I looked over to Josh, and I could see she did not like this kid. Josh went through her normal routine and wound up and threw the ball in. I could tell as soon as it left her hand it was a wild ball. It hit the ground to the right of Alex. She had to jump up to grab the ball.

The ump yelled out, "BALL!"

Ronny tipped his helmet back a little and yelled out to Josh, "Maybe we need to get your freak brother out here to pitch for you."

That comment shocked the fans as well as the players. You could hear some booing from the bleachers. Josh did not take it lightly. She was already in a bad mood, and this put her over the top.

She threw her glove down and charged at Ronny. I think it was more than he expected. He started backing down as she came at him. I knew I needed to do something. I ran out to grab her as fast as I could. I reached her about five feet in front of the base. The ump had worked his way around to get in between the two players.

"Coach, you need to control your player," he insisted.

I had Josh in my grasp, but she was still trying to get to Ronny.

"Sorry, Blue," I said.

I turned her around and started walking her back to the mound. I looked back at the stands. Most of the people were up on their feet, including the adoptive parents. I could almost read their faces as they watched me take her back. We stopped just short of the mound, and I made her look at me.

"Hey, come here. Don't let him get to you."

She didn't say anything. She just looked back at Ronny with a glare of hatred.

"Hey, look at me! What's going on with you?"

She turned her gaze to me and softened a little.

"Nothing. I'm fine."

I kept looking at her, waiting for more.

"I'm fine. Let's just play."

With that, she turned away from me and picked up her glove. I walked back to the bench. Lisa was looking at me with a very concerned look. Miss Esther reached over and rubbed Cody on the head. Cody just seemed to take it in stride. I am sure this was not the first time that he had been the subject of childish teasing.

The game continued, but again the team was not playing with the usual zest they normally did. Josh's pitching was falling off. She was walking a lot of players. The defense was doing well so we were able to hold them to six points. We were still down by two, but I still felt like we had a chance. I wished Josh could get out of this funk she was in.

We had two outs, and Ronny Martin was up again. I watched Josh as he walked up. This time she didn't seem to mind. She was smiling at Alex. I glanced over to Alex, and she had a big smile on her face as well. She reached over and patted her right thigh three times and then put her mask back on. Josh nodded her head and smirked. What were these two up to?

Just Believe

Josh got into her windup. I could tell she was going to throw a fastball by the way she was standing. She cranked way back and let it fly. It was one of the fastest balls I had ever seen her throw. You could hear it whizzing through the air as it went and then all you could hear was a hard **thud** as the ball crashed into Ronny Martin's left thigh. Bam! He went down like a ton of bricks.

The ump cried out "Dead ball. Take your base."

I was upset, "JOSH!"

I looked over at the ump and called time out. Josh looked over to me with a sheepish look and then turned away. I trotted out to the mound. Again, many of the fans were on their feet, and again the adoptive parents were looking at each other. I am sure they were wondering why this sweet kid was lashing out like she was.

I got to the mound. "Josh, turn around and look at me." She did, slowly, but she would not make eye contact. "Josh, come on talk to me!"

Then she reared up and almost yelled at me, "What do you care?"

"What do I care? Josh, what is going on with you?" I asked.

She just looked at me, now with sadness in her eyes. "It doesn't matter anyhow. After this game is over, you won't have to put up with me anymore."

"Josh, I'm not putting up with you, I…"

Just then, the ump called out from his position behind the base. "Coach, let's play ball!"

When I looked back at Josh, she had turned away from me and was throwing the ball into her glove.

The Big Game

"Josh, I am not sure what you are thinking, but I am not *putting up* with you. It's not like that."

I backed up a few steps and then turned and walked back to our bench. She kicked the dirt on the mound a little and then got ready to play again.

I could tell the ump was getting tired of dealing with all of this.

"Let's play ball, folks!" he yelled out.

We were able to hold them to just six points over the next two innings. Then the score was tied up, mostly because our defense was playing a great game. It was the last inning, and it was our turn to bat. We needed one more run to win. In this league, they do not play tiebreakers. A tie goes to the team with the best ranking. If we wanted this thing, we had to win it in this inning. Jason got up and hit a nice pop fly to center field. The outfielder made a great diving catch.

"OUT!" the ump yelled.

Next up was Jimmy, our shortstop. He had been having a rough year with batting, so I was concerned.

"Come on, Jimmy, you can do it. Nobody better," I yelled as he was getting up to bat. The first ball came in hard and fast.

"Strike!" the ump yelled out.

"That's OK, buddy, you can do it," I yelled to him. The second ball came in, and he hit it hard. It went just over the shortstop's head. He stood there for a second, almost as if he didn't believe he hit it.

"Run! *Run!*" I yelled.

Just Believe

He took off running for first base. I was watching the left fielder. He was bobbling the ball a little.

"Take two," I yelled at Jimmy, as he was rounding first. He took off for second base, and I was yelling at the top of my lungs. "GO, GO, GO!"

Every person in the stands was on their feet. It looked like he was going to make it. The left fielder had the ball and threw it with all his might. Jimmy was running for everything he had. It was going to be close.

"Slide! Slide! *Slide!*" I screamed at him.

Jimmy went down into a slide. The ball was coming in fast. The second base player caught the ball and whipped her arm down hard, just catching the tip of Jimmy's shoelace as he slid in.

"OUT!" the ump cried sharply.

A collective moan came from the bleachers. Jimmy was crushed.

"That's OK. You'll get it next time."

I looked over at the team. I could see they were ready to give up. I looked over at the ump and gave him the time-out sign.

All the players were sitting on the bench as Jimmy came in and sat down. He was visibly defeated. Josh was sitting on the far end of the bench with Eddy's glove in her lap, staring at the ground. She didn't acknowledge any of the other players. I knew I needed to do something. Then Charles' words came to me: "Now that you know the truth, you must pass it on."

Now was the time. I looked at the team for a second and then said, "OK, team, this is it. We've got two outs, and we only need one run to win. You have all played a beautiful game against the best team in the league, and they are not going to just hand this to us."

I paced back and forth. They were all listening to me attentively, except for Josh.

"You know there are things that happen in life that are out of our control. That is just the way life is. We may not be able to control what is going on around us, but what we can control is ourselves. We get to choose how we respond to what life throws at us. We get to choose to believe that anything is possible. Even if it looks like things aren't going to happen the way we hoped they would."

I caught Josh's eye on that last sentence. I think she knew what I was talking about.

"The question is, are you willing to believe? Are you willing to believe that anything is possible if you believe it is?"

I paused for effect. It looked like I was getting through to them. Lisa was watching me and had a big smile on her face. I looked down at Alex.

"Alex, do you believe?"

"Yes," she said.

Then I looked over to Jimmy.

"Jimmy, do you believe?"

Jimmy yelled, "Yes!"

Then I looked at Jason. By this time I was yelling.

"Jason, do you believe?"

"Yes!" he screamed back at me.

Just Believe

Now we were on a roll. "Tigers," I yelled out, "do you believe?"

"Yes," they screamed back at me.

"What? I *can't* hear you!"

"Yes!" they yelled even louder.

Everyone except Josh that is.

"One more time!" I encouraged.

"Yes!" came the reply to me loud and clear.

"OK! Let's go out and get them!"

Then from behind me, I heard Josh speak up. "Coach, do you really believe?"

She looked at me with eyes that were searching for answers.

"Yes, Josh, I believe in you!"

It was true. I did believe in that little girl with all the hope for the future. I truly wanted what was best for her, and if the best was these adoptive parents, I could live with that. She could see in my eyes that I was not lying. She knew I did truly believe.

I turned back to the team and said, "Come on, team! Let's hear that Tiger **roar** and go win this game."

They all lifted their hands up in the shape of claws and let out a loud **ROAR!** It was great.

I looked over at Lisa, and she gave me a big smile of approval. I could tell she was happy to have her old husband back again.

Then out of the corner of my eye, standing alongside the bleachers next to Miss Esther was the unmistakable shape of Charles. He took a half step forward and tipped his hat to me. Then he gave me that huge grin of his and let out a little chuckle. I looked back to Lisa to see if she had seen him. I got her attention and pointed to where he was standing, but when I looked back, he was gone. I just saw Miss Esther and the other kids sitting around her. Lisa looked over, saw Miss Esther, and then looked back at me wondering why I was pointing at her. I had to laugh. Lisa looked at me, and then shook her head and went back to talking with her friend Deb.

Charles had to know that I was sharing The Message that he had given to me with the kids. I am sure he was proud.

It was Josh's turn to bat.

"Josh, you're up," I called out.

She met me at the opening of the fence at our bench. She had a look of confidence on her face, and she was smiling from ear to ear. She was back. I bent over to talk with her.

"Watch the inside pitch. Step back from the plate a little."

"OK."

She turned and walked toward home plate.

The crowd was going wild. This was it. A tied game with two outs. You could feel excitement in the air.

Josh walked past the stands, and Lisa yelled out to her: "Come on, Josh! Knock it outta here!"

Lisa's friend Deb was cheering next to her. "Let's go, Josh! You can do it!"

Josh looked up and smiled. The adoptive couple looked on with anticipation. Josh stepped up to the plate.

Just Believe

The first pitch came in hard and fast, just missing her by an inch. It was a message from the pitcher.

"Ball," the ump called out. He then lifted his mask and spoke to the pitcher: "Let's keep this a friendly game."

Josh looked up at me, remembering what I told her. She took half a step back from the plate and then got set to receive the ball. The next ball came in fast again, but I knew she had this one. She reared back and swung with all of her might. **CRACK!**

I always loved the sound of a bat hitting a baseball, but this time it was extra special. She had really connected with the ball and it was gone. The crowd erupted, and she took off running. The ball went over the left fielder's head, and he was running to retrieve it.

"Go for two!" I yelled at her as she got to first base. She kept running and clearly was going to be safe on second. She was about three feet from the bag when the outfielder threw the ball in. He threw it wide and completely missed the second base player.

I screamed like a schoolboy, "Go for three! Go for three!"

She took off running and was safe at third. The first baseman had the ball and was walking it in to the center of the infield.

"Time!" the ump cried out.

The crowd went crazy. What a great time for a triple!

Alex was up next. She was never one of our strongest hitters, but I wanted her to go for it.

The Big Game

"Wait for the right pitch. Take your time. They are more nervous about you than you are about them."

She nodded and swallowed hard.

"Now go get 'em!"

The crowd was cheering her on as she walked up. She was clearly nervous.

"Come on, Alex! You can do this," Josh yelled out from third base.

Alex took her position at the plate and put the bat up on her shoulder. That made me a little nervous. The first pitch came in. She swung at it wildly and completely missed.

"Strike!" came the call from the ump.

I had to do something. I got her attention as she stepped out of the batter's box. I tipped my hat to her, which told her I was going to give her a sign. *Now watch me* was all I could think. One tug on the hat, a slide down the left arm, and a tug on the right ear. The first two signs didn't mean anything. It was what I did all the time. The tug on the ear was the sign—BUNT! Hopefully she got it. She said she did when she nodded to me, and I gave her a big smile.

OK, here we go, I thought to myself.

Alex settled back into the batter's box. The pitcher got the sign from the catcher and nodded his head. He wound up and tossed in a nice curveball. Alex quickly put her bat out in front of her. Josh was already about ten feet off the base ready to go. The ball almost floated in to her. She leaned into it and **Thud**—the ball hit her bat and bounced straight down to the ground. It was perfect.

Just Believe

The field was a scurry of movement. Alex took off running for the first. The catcher and the pitcher were both running for the ball while Josh took off from third heading for home. The ball bounced forward about 10 feet and stopped.

Josh was halfway to home plate. The pitcher got to the ball, but the catcher was off the bag because he was running after the ball. He quickly changed direction and was headed back to home plate to try to get Josh out.

Alex was on fire. She crossed first base and had turned around to watch the action at home. Josh was now about five feet from the home plate bag. The pitcher had picked up the ball and threw it to the catcher who was still back-pedaling to get to the bag. Josh went into a slide as the catcher caught the ball. It was down to the wire.

The catcher thrust his glove at Josh hoping to hit her before she got to the bag. There was a big dust cloud raised from the slide.

Josh was lying still. The catcher was lying on his back with the glove up over his head. It was completely silent. The dust started to settle as the umpire was standing right over the base. As the air cleared, he could see the result of the slide.

"SAFE!" he yelled out.

The crowd erupted with screams of delight. I grabbed Alex, and we hugged as we ran to home plate. Josh got up and ran to me. She jumped in my arms, and we hugged. The whole bench had cleared, and we were all jumping up and down. This was moment number six etched in my memory.

The Big Game

After the short celebration, we shook hands with the other team, and then we were awarded the trophy. The adoptive parents came over to me and thanked me for all I had done to help Josh. Miss Esther had told them about our relationship.

"You're welcome," is all I could say.

I wanted to say so much more, but I just congratulated them and walked over to Lisa. We watched together as the caseworker got Josh's bag from Miss Esther, and Josh walked away with her new family. As she walked away, she looked back at Lisa and me and then over to Miss Esther and Rachael.

Rachael ran to Josh and hugged her. "I don't want you to go, Josh," she cried.

Josh was as brave as any little girl could be in this situation. She held Rachael out at arm's length and spoke to her.

"Rachael, now listen to me. Crying isn't going to make this any better. I have to go now, but we will see each other again."

As she said this, she looked over at Lisa and me and said, "Rachael, we need to Just Believe." She held my gaze for a moment and then she turned as Miss Esther came over to get Rachael. By the look on the adoptive parents' faces, I could see that they were not aware of the relationship between Josh and Rachael.

She was so brave, and I was so proud of her.

The ride home was pretty quiet. Neither of us had much to say, though we both knew what we were each thinking about. When we got home, I took all of the gear and put it away in the garage as Lisa went in the house to make dinner. We sat at the table and ate our meal in silence for the most part until Lisa asked, "What are you thinking about?" It took me a second to formulate my thoughts.

"I can't believe she will be gone tomorrow," I said.

"There is nothing you could have done," Lisa reassured.

"I could have at least tried, but I was afraid."

"Afraid? Of what?"

I knew this was not the right way to think, but it was what was going through my head and my heart. "That in some way, if I were to love another child, I would be cheating...on Eddy," I confessed.

"Stanley, honey, I believe you have enough love in your heart to keep what you have for Eddy and to love another child, too."

"But I don't want to love 'another' child. I want to love Josh...and now it's too late. I should have done something, but I didn't."

I got up and took my plate to the kitchen and put it in the sink. I was trying to figure this whole thing out. In my heart, I wanted Josh to be our child.

Charles told me that anything was possible if I believed it was. I wanted to believe it was possible, but this was new territory for me. My old thinking kept trying to creep its way into my head. I kept getting hit with feelings of anger again. Thoughts of blaming others for Josh leaving kept rising in my head.

I stood at the kitchen sink having a battle in my brain until I told the thought to be silent. I spoke softly to myself. *I choose to believe.* That was it. I felt peace come over me. It really worked. I could choose how I wanted to think. I could choose to be peaceful and not let the thoughts that come to me control me. I could believe, and all things could become possible to me. It was a revelation.

I went back out into the dining room. Lisa was cleaning up the table from dinner. I grabbed a couple of items.

"Oh yeah, I almost forgot. Do you remember when I was trying to get your attention at the game? I pointed over toward Miss Esther?"

"Yes. I still don't know what you were pointing at. She was at the game the whole time."

"Yeah, I know, but I wasn't pointing at her. I was pointing at Charles. He was standing right next to her." She stared at me in disbelief.

"When I gave the kids the pep talk, I looked over at you, and then I noticed him standing there."

"What did he do? Did he say anything?" Lisa asked.

"No. He tipped his hat to me, and then he gave me a huge smile. When I tried to get your attention so you could see him, he was gone. I hate it when he does that."

"Wow! That is great. I wonder why he was there," she said.

"I don't know. I was thinking it was because I was sharing The Message with the kids. Do you remember when he told us that we needed to share it with others?"

"Maybe he was letting you know you were on the right track."

We continued to clear the dishes and turned in early for the night.

The next morning, Lisa didn't have any clients for the day, and I was ahead on my writing, so we decided, as the final event for our newly cleaned and organized garage, to install a garage door opener since we could now actually park our car in it. I was up on a ladder tightening the last bolts on it when Lisa came in with a nice cold glass of tea.

"Looks great in here," she said as she handed me the drink.

"Thanks. Watch this." I reached over to the button on the wall and pushed it.

As I did, the garage door opener kicked into gear and the door slowly closed. Lisa smiled big.

"Nice."

I hit the button again and the door slowly opened. As the garage door opened, it revealed Austin, Miss Esther's oldest foster son, standing in the driveway. He had the glove that I had given Josh in his hands.

"Hey Austin, come on in," I called out.

He stepped into the garage, and I could tell he had something to say.

"What is it, bud?" I said to him.

"Uh, Mr. Walters? Josh gave this to me and asked me to give it to you."

He handed me the glove. I could tell this was not a message that he wanted to deliver.

"Thanks, bud," I said to him, and he turned and walked out.

I looked over at Lisa and she just shrugged her shoulders. There really wasn't anything to say at this moment.

I walked to the back of the garage and put the glove in a box up on a shelf. It was the same box that Josh had taken the glove out of several weeks before. It was the box marked *Eddy's Stuff.* That box held all of the items that we had left of our son. We were ready to move on, not forget him mind you, but make room for other love in our lives.

I put the glove in the box and stood there for a moment. I was sad, but this time it was different. I was sad without the anger. I wanted Josh to be a part of our lives, but I didn't know what to do. I turned around and looked at Lisa.

"Honey, I need your help here. I feel like it is over, but I don't want it to be. I want to have that little girl be a part of our lives."

"Stanley, maybe Josh won't be a part of our lives. Maybe she came along to help you heal and to show you that you *could* love again."

"Maybe you're right. I don't know," I replied.

She walked over to me and took my hands in hers.

"How about this. What if we do what Charles told us to do?"

I wasn't sure what she meant, and I am sure my face showed that clearly.

"What if we choose to believe that the right child, or children, will come to us at the right time in our lives."

I was amazed at how smart this beautiful lady was.

"You're right," I said. "I am willing to just believe that we will have the children that we need who also need to be with us."

I leaned over and kissed her.

"Lisa, my dear, you are an amazing woman"

She smiled at me, and we went into the house. As we walked up the back porch stairs, I hit the remote and the garage door closed. I stopped at the top of the stairs and watched it for a moment and felt as though a door of my past, especially the past two years, was also being shut, and the future was mine to be had. Life was good again.

Lisa and I had decided to run some errands in the afternoon. We were just getting ready to walk out the door when the phone rang. I was surprised to hear it was Bernice, Josh's caseworker, on the other end.

"Hello, Bernice, is there something I can help you with?"

"Mr. Walters, do think it would be possible for you to come down to the office this afternoon?"

"I guess so. Is there something wrong?" I asked.

"No. Everything is fine. I want to see if you would be willing to help me with a project."

I looked over at Lisa who could hear both sides of the conversation. "Uh, sure we can come right over," I told her.

I was about to hang up when she added, "Oh, and Mr. Walters, could you bring Cooper with you and the glove that you gave to Josh?"

Lisa and I just looked at each other for a second, and I said, "Sure. We'll see you in a little bit."

When we arrived, we met with Bernice and made one of the biggest and best decisions we had ever made in our lives.

After that, we were asked to sit in the waiting room. From where we were, we could see Josh sitting in the conference room through the glass. Her back was to us, so she did not know we were there. She was sitting alone in a chair at the end of the table. The table was free of any items except for one office phone.

Josh seemed withdrawn and upset.

Bernice told us to wait until she called for us. She said we would know what to do.

Bernice then entered the conference room with a stack of papers and put them down on the table. She sat down and looked at Josh, who was sitting with her arms folded and staring down at the table.

"So, this is the big day. How do you feel?" she asked.

We could hear Bernice clearly from where we were sitting.

Josh didn't answer her; she continued to stare at the table.

"Joscelyn, please talk to me."

Josh slowly looked up at her and paused for a moment. Bernice waited for her to speak.

"I want to go back to Miss Esther's," she said.

"Josh, this family is very nice, and they want to make this work."

Josh was defiant now.

"I don't care. If I can't go back to Miss Esther's, then I don't want to go anywhere."

Bernice gave her a slight smile and then picked up the phone.

"Well, we'll see about that."

Josh folded her arms again and went back to staring at the table.

Bernice was right. We knew what to do. I took the glove out and gave it to Cooper and said, "Go see Josh, buddy."

He walked to the conference room as if he knew what was going on from the beginning. He stepped into the doorway with the baseball glove in his mouth and let out a little groan. Josh looked up, and it seemed that she couldn't believe her eyes. Then she said, "Cooper!" as only an excited little ten-year-old girl can do.

Josh grabbed the glove out of his mouth and then hugged him. She was in another place. She wasn't even thinking about what was going on around her. She was just glad to see her friend Cooper. Then she stopped and looked over to Bernice.

"What is Cooper doing here?"

"He came with the Walters"

As she said that, Lisa and I stepped in the doorway. Josh looked over at us with a total look of bewilderment. Then she looked over at Bernice.

"The Walters are looking to adopt," explained Bernice. That statement was strange for us to hear. It was what we wanted and what we agreed to do, but it was still a surprise to us.

Josh snapped her head back around to us.

"You guys are looking to adopt a kid?" she asked.

It was fun to watch. Her little brain was clicking away, but she just wasn't getting it.

Lisa stepped in the room and spoke up, "Well, not just any kid."

I took a step up next to Lisa.

"Yeah, Josh, we were wondering if you would consider coming to live with us." I said.

"You mean like a foster kid?"

Lisa replied, "No. More like a daughter."

Josh looked back to Bernice and then back to us. It was all beginning to click now. She started to get a big smile on her face, and then I jumped in again.

"There is one thing you will need to consider before you give us your answer," I explained.

She was surprised by this. "What?" she asked.

"You would have to share a room with your sister," I said.

Josh quickly came back, "I don't have a sister."

As she said that, Alice walked in with Rachael at her side. Lisa and I stepped aside and Rachael, toting her burned bunny, stepped between us.

Josh exploded out of her chair.

"Rachael!" she screamed.

Rachael was equally enthusiastic.

"Josh!"

The two of them hugged for a moment, and then we all hugged.

Just Believe

Bernice chimed in, "So, Josh, do you think you might want to live with the Walters after all?"

"Yes! I really want to live with them," Josh said.

We were all a bunch of smiles and hugs.

"I thought you might change your mind," Bernice said. "OK, girls. I need you to go with Miss Alice while Mr. and Mrs. Walters and I talk some more."

Josh and Rachael walked out of the room holding hands as they went. Lisa and I looked at each other for a moment and then sat down at the table opposite Bernice. Bernice opened the folder and started going through some papers that we would need to read and sign.

Then I heard a knock on the door. It was Josh. She was standing in the doorway.

"Ah, Mr. Stan?" I got up out of my chair and walked over to her.

"What is it, honey?" I asked her.

She looked me straight in the eyes as only she can do. I bent down to be even with her.

"Thank you," she said.

"For what?" I responded.

"For believing in me," she said.

I was taken aback by her statement. For believing in her? I thought to myself, *She is easy to believe in.*

"No, Josh," I said. "Thank you for believing in me."

This is moment number seven that will forever be etched in my memory.

She reached up and grabbed me around the neck and we hugged for a moment. When we pulled away, she laughed at me because I had a tear in my eye.

The Big Game

"Allergies!" I said. "Now get out of here. We have work to do."

She smiled at me and turned around and walked away. I wiped my eyes and went back to the table. Lisa smiled at me as I sat down.

"Thank you for doing all of this for us," I said to Bernice.

"Don't thank *me*. When the adoptive parents saw you at the game with Josh, they knew you had to be together."

I picked up the papers and started to sign them.

Lisa was watching us and then glanced over to her left. Sitting on the table was Rachael's burnt bunny. She reached over and picked it up. She glanced over at the doorway and then smiled. *I guess she won't need this anymore*, she thought to herself.

That is the story of how I lost my life and then gained it back through a simple principle of believing. Those two simple words—*just believe*— are full of so much power. If we were able to grasp just a small understanding of them, we would all be living the lives we want to live. It has been proven in my life.

You might think my story ends here. On the contrary, this is where it actually begins.

Chapter Twelve

Personal Initiative

"When you believe in what you're doing and use your imagination and initiative, you can make a difference."

Samuel Dash

Six months passed since I *had* last saw Charles. Josh and Rachael adapted well to living with Lisa and me. I became so attached to the both of them you would never have known that they were not my natural-born children.

Lisa was promoted to manager at the gym. She loved working there, and she was able to set her hours so she could take the girls to school in the morning and then work during the middle of the day. I usually picked the girls up from school, and we would cook dinner together.

Rachael really took a liking to cooking and had quickly become one of the most talkative little girls you could ever meet. She still had dreams of her mom and dad, but she was at a place where she could talk about them with us. She had come to terms with losing them. At least as much as an eight-year-old child can.

Just Believe

Miss Esther was still living next to us. Austin and Cody found permanent homes, and she had three new kids living with her. We spent a lot of time with her and the kids she watched.

Bernice has asked us several different times to visit with prospective adopting parents. I enjoy these visits because I am able to share The Message of *"Just Believe"* with these people. It is a remarkable message really. So simple and yet so full of life. I have seen this message change people's lives, and I am grateful for it.

I was as busy as I wanted to be with writing for technical manuals. I was still working on the book you are reading, *Just Believe*. I wanted to make sure I did The Message justice.

Time flies, and it was already time for spring practice. I wanted to get a jump-start with the team, so I called an early practice. All of the kids from the year before showed up. It was almost like a class reunion. They were all jazzed and ready to play again. Coming off of the previous year's win had them pumped to play again that year. We had a few new recruits.

On this afternoon, we put in a couple of hours of drills just to get the rust out. While we were playing, I noticed the groundskeeper, Sam, mowing the grass on the backside of the field. The last time I had talked with him, I was very rude and yelled at him. I am embarrassed when I think about it now.

I sent all the kids home, including Josh and Rachael. I wanted to talk with him to set things right. I gathered all of our gear and put it in the back of my SUV. I walked over to the back of the fields. On the far left side of the field, there is a building that has restrooms on one side and a maintenance shed on the other. Sam was putting some gear away and had his back to me when I walked up.

"Ahem," I cleared my throat to get his attention.

He turned around and I realized it wasn't Sam.

"Uh, excuse me, I don't mean to bother you. Can you tell me if Sam still works here?"

"Sam?" he asked with a confused look on his face.

"Yes. He was the groundskeeper here last year." I said.

He turned to face me fully, took off his hat, and scratched his head. "Don't know how that could be. I've been the only groundskeeper here for the past three years. You sure you got the right fields?"

"Yes," I said as I pointed to the bleachers. "I sat and talked with him right over there on those benches."

He put his hat back on and walked out of the shed to see where I was pointing.

"Well, I don't know what to tell ya, friend. Like I said, I took this job over three years ago from a guy named Evan who worked here for almost 15 years before me."

"Yes. I remember Evan from when I played here before," I replied.

He stood there and smiled at me.

"Well, thanks for your help; sorry to bother you." I said.

He smiled at me.

"Was no bother really. Hope you can find your friend."

I walked back to my SUV and sat in the front seat for a second. *So where did Sam go?* Or *Where did he come from?* might be the right question.

I closed the driver's door and started the engine. I put the car in reverse and I looked in the rearview mirror. There, plain as day, Charles was sitting in my back seat.

"Hello, Stanley," he said with a smile.

"Ahh!" is all that came out of me. He startled me.

I put the car in park and hopped out. I did it so fast I forgot to turn the engine off.

I stood outside the car as Charles slowly opened the back door and climbed out. He put his hat on his head and took a deep breath in. He held it for a second and then let it out with a nice long sigh.

"AHHHHHH. I love the smell of spring, don't you?"

I had to take all of this in for a moment. He was back. What did this mean? Would he tell me more? I was full of questions. He looked at me a little more intently.

"Don't you love the smell of spring, Stanley?" he asked.

"Ah, yes. Yes, I do. It's my favorite time of year."

He smiled big and said, "The beginning of baseball season, I know."

He started to walk back toward the fields.

"Walk with me, Stanley. I have some things to talk to you about."

I complied and stepped in right next to him.

"Stanley," he said, "you have been doing well for yourself.

"You have grasped the power of The Message, and you have been sharing it with others."

I looked up at him as we walked. "You have gained the attention of some of the powers that be, and I have been instructed to talk with you," he said.

"Talk with me? Am I in trouble?"

He chuckled. "No, Stanley. On the contrary, you have within you the makings of a great messenger. The question is, are you willing?"

We worked our way to the back of the field and stopped at the bleachers that Sam and I sat on when I met him. He pointed to me to have a seat. We both sat down, side by side.

"Willing?" I asked.

"Yes, Stanley. This is no small commitment. To be a messenger, it must be your whole life. You have to be willing to give up everything that you want and be willing to focus on everyone else around you."

He paused for a moment to let it all sink in.

"Don't be too alarmed my friend. You will find that when your focus is on helping other people, your life will be so fulfilled that any dreams and wishes you may have thought you wanted will pale in comparison."

This all sounded so amazing I didn't know what to think.

"Stanley, you may not have noticed, but you already started when you took those two girls into your home and loved them as your own. That is what a messenger does."

I couldn't help but smile when the girls were brought up.

"Did you lose anything when you did that?"

"No," I responded quickly. "Just the opposite. I couldn't picture life without them," I said.

"When you meet with other adoptive parents and you teach them what you have learned with The Message and with raising your girls, do you lose anything by sharing that time with them?"

Again I had to answer, "No. I get great pleasure out of sharing with them and helping them. I have also made some great friends in doing it."

He nodded his head at my statement.

"That is the life of a messenger: spreading The Message of *'Just believe'* to all that you meet; going out of your way to help other people; and looking for opportunity to change the world around you, one person at a time."

I didn't know what to say. He could tell I was on the edge of my seat.

"Stanley, this is no small commitment. The Message will be your life, and your life will be The Message. Are you sure you are up for that?"

I looked away from him for a moment as I thought to myself. Of course this is what I wanted. The message that he brought to me in my darkest hour saved me. How could I not want to do the same for others?

I turned and looked at him.

"Yes, I am ready. I want to become a messenger."

He smiled that big smile of his. I couldn't help but smile back to him.

Then it occurred to me. "Oh wait, will I get special powers like you? You know appear and disappear and all?"

Charles let out a hearty laugh. I had to wait a few moments until the laughter subsided.

"You are a special one, aren't you? Stanley, messengers come in all forms. There are thousands of people living on the earth today who have received The Message just as you have. They are ordinary people living their lives just as you are. The only difference is that they have made a commitment to stop living for themselves and start living for others. There are only a few like me. We are the overseers of The Message. You actually have met one of my counterparts."

I thought to myself for a moment.

"Sam?" I asked.

"Yes. Sam was actually a messenger on Earth for many years until he left this place and came to join my ranks. Sam was actually one of the foremost authorities on The Message, and his work is still changing people's lives."

I didn't know what to say.

"Now listen to me closely, Stanley. You have already received the first principle of The Message when you grasped the power of just believe. There are actually ten principles to this message, and if a person were able to apply just one of them to their life, it would be the difference between living an extraordinary life or a life of mediocrity.

"This first principle that you have been exposed to is the principle that is the driving force behind the phrase *just believe*. It is the principle of faith. You see, Stanley, it all starts with the willingness to believe that something is possible.

"In my favorite book, my friend Paul says that faith is the substance of things hoped for and yet unseen. Faith is the future in front of you waiting to be discovered. Nothing is formed on this earth without it first being thought of. You have to have faith. The opposite of faith is fear, doubt, and worry. Those three things can turn a molehill into a mountain. Faith has the ability to remove any mountain.

"Think back to when we first met, and I said the words *Just believe* to you. You didn't understand what I was saying, did you?"

"No," I replied.

"But, what you didn't know is that I was planting a seed in you. It was a seed of faith. When you were able to start believing, or having faith, you started this force in motion. Faith is a force that, once in motion, cannot be stopped. You see it every day. You just don't realize it. Faith is the key that allows us to put things into action.

"Listen to me for a moment, Stanley. There is a distinguishable difference between people who are successful in life and those who are not. It is their capacity for belief. The failures will see the hole in the doughnut, but will not see the doughnut around the hole. The successful people see the hole in the doughnut, but see the doughnut as well.

"Many people have a plan or idea that would be very useful to the world around them, but they lack the self-confidence or faith to do it. Belief is truly a magical word, because it is the beginning of all success. It is the very foundation of civilization; it is the one quality you must make use of before you can get an understanding of The Message. Without faith, it is pointless. Faith sees things where others see nothing. Faith believes when others say there is nothing to believe. Without faith, the other principles of The Message are pointless. Faith is the greatest gift that we have been given. It is how we create our lives into what we want them to be."

He paused for a moment to let all of what he said sink in. Then he looked at me and gave me a wink. I was trying to soak it all in. How could I remember all of this?

As if he knew what I was thinking, he looked at me and said, "Have faith, Stanley. You will be a great force in delivering this message."

"In the next few weeks you are going to meet other messengers who will share with you the ten principles of The Message. Some are overseers like I am; others are living on the earth right now. Listen to them when they talk with you. Use your gift and write it down. Most importantly, share it with others."

Again, I stared at him as if he was speaking a foreign language to me.

"So, Stanley, are you sure this is something you want to do?"

I knew the answer before he asked me the question. I am pretty sure he knew it, too.

"Yes, I want to do it. I am just concerned about having the ability to do it," I admitted.

"Trust me, Stanley, you are going to do fine, as long as you are willing to believe you are."

I smiled at him, and he smiled back.

I had a head full of questions I had to get answered before he left.

"How will I know who the messengers are? Can I tell Lisa about this? Should I quit my job?"

He held up his cane to stop me.

"Stanley, you will know when you meet them. Yes, please tell Lisa, and no, this is not a job. It is your life. When you are a messenger, your work will reflect your life.

"There is one more thing that you will need to consider while you are meeting with all of the other messengers. It is imperative that you discover your definite major purpose."

I jumped in. "My major purpose?"

"Yes, Stanley. It is that one thing that defines you. It is that thing that you would do no matter if you were paid to do it or not. It is that one thing that says to you, 'This is who I am.'"

He paused for a moment as I tried to let this sink in.

"You will recognize it when it presents itself. Definite major purposes are something that are created through discovering who you really are way deep down inside. Most people fill their days with busy work. They do what they feel is necessary to exist in this world. There are only a few who have discovered their definite major purpose and are living in that realm. You know who they are when you meet them. They have a sense of peace and confidence that exudes from them, and in most cases, they are working to help others fulfill their dreams.

"When you identify your definite major purpose, it will be the most natural thing you have ever experienced in your life. You will find that all that you have been taught about work and dreams will fight you. You will need to renew your mind and change your thinking. This will bring you total fulfillment in life and a peace that will pass all understanding."

I was thinking this to myself, but I think the words came out. "My definite major purpose."

Charles smiled at me and then stood up.

"Now, I must be on my way. Trust me, Stanley. All of your questions will be answered in due time."

Just then, the groundskeeper fired up the Weed Wacker behind me, and I turned to look at him. As I did, it made me think of one more question.

"So, was Sam a groundskeeper when he was on ear..."

I turned as I was asking the question, and Charles was gone. I sat there on the bench talking to myself for who knows how long. Then the thought came to me about Josh's comment in the garage: *the crazy dog guy*. Now it made sense to me. Ha! I had to laugh at myself.

A week went by after my meeting with Charles. I was in a strange state because I kept expecting him to show up wherever I went. One time in the grocery store, I was walking down the bread aisle, and I saw a man with a hat that looked just like the one Charles wore. He was on the other side of the aisle.

"Charles," I called out to him, but he didn't stop.

I caught up to him and grabbed him by the arm.

"Charles, it's me," I said as I stopped him.

Of course, it wasn't him, and by the look on the nice gentleman's face, I was about one step from being arrested.

"Sorry," is all I could say.

I decided to stop looking for him and just wait until he came back to see me. Little did I know that he would return just a few days later.

The next day, I was on my morning walk with Cooper. Lisa was at work and the girls were at school. Cooper and I loved to walk down to Woodward Park in the mornings. Woodward is one of those old city parks that are timeless. It has a creek that runs down the middle of it and a beautiful wooded area that is totally cleared out except for an old grove of oak trees. As is our tradition when we get to the trees, I let Cooper go to run free. He loves to play with the squirrels.

As I was walking along watching Cooper play, I saw a man sitting on one of the benches dressed in a khaki shirt and pants. I didn't really pay much attention to him until I got closer. He was reading the newspaper and didn't pay much attention to me either until I got within a few steps from him. He put the paper down and looked up at me. It was Sam.

"Good morning, Stanley," he said to me.

"Sam! How are you? I didn't expect to see you," I replied.

"I am good, Stanley. It is good to see you."

Cooper came running up to greet Sam.

"Hello Cooper. How have you been?"

He gave him a couple pats on the head and then got right down to business.

"Stanley, as you know, you have been selected to become one of the messengers. I can't tell you how pleased I am to hear that. From the first time I saw you, I knew you would be a great candidate."

I interrupted, "Sam, I wanted to talk to you about that. I was very rude to you, and I want to say that I am sorry for that way I acted."

He smiled big at me. "No need to apologize, Stan. I totally understand where you were with your thinking at that time."

Then he continued, "Coming back to what I was saying. Your journey will start today. You are going to meet other people who have received The Message and are now messengers themselves. Let me give you one word of advice as you take this journey: Take a pen and paper with you. I like to carry a journal with me."

He reached over and held up an old leather journal much like the one Charles had in our kitchen.

"Make sure to write down what you hear. There is a power released in the universe when you write thoughts down. They go from just being a thought in your mind to a physical tangible item. This is how you create. You take a thought, and you write it down."

I looked at him and then at his journal. Of course I didn't have one with me.

"OK, I'll get one right away," I said.

He smiled at me and then went on. "Today, you are going to meet one of my favorite messengers. He will be waiting for you at his favorite restaurant, Ti Amo's over on Sheridan. Go there at 12 noon sharp. He will be waiting for you," he said.

"How will I know who he is?" I asked.

Sam let out a little chuckle and then said, "Trust me. He will see you before you see him."

I went home after that meeting. It was now 11:00 A.M. I had an hour to pick up a journal. I arrived at Ti Amo's five minutes before noon just as Sam had said. I brought with me three pens and my new journal. I wanted to be prepared for what this messenger had to say.

I walked in the front door of the restaurant. It was a nicely complemented Italian eatery with a large dining room on the left side. In the middle, as you walked in, was a U-shaped bar, and on the right side were several meeting rooms that I assume were used for larger parties. One of those rooms had a set of French doors on it that led to a beautiful boardroom setting. It was all wood paneling with a very nice, large table in the middle that looked like it sat about ten people.

I stood in Ti Amo's entranceway for a second. Then I noticed the doors to the boardroom open. An attractive woman with long dark hair came walking up to me.

"Hello. My name is Kelly. You must be Stanley," she said.

"Ah, yes," I said as I shook her hand.

"Please follow me," she said as she turned and walked back toward the boardroom.

As we entered the room, I could see a man sitting on the left side of the table. He was a distinguished-looking man who appeared to be in his early 50s. He stood as we entered the room.

"Hello, Stanley," he said as he reached out his hand to shake mine. "My name is Jim Stovall. You have met my colleague, Kelly."

"Yes," I said as I reached out to shake his hand, and as I did, I noticed something. He did not move his hand to meet mine as most do when shaking. I grasped his hand, and we shook.

"Please, sit down," he said as he motioned to my chair.

I sat down in silence, trying to take the room in. I was looking around the room when he spoke again.

"Well, Stanley, we should get right to it."

As he said this, a waiter walked in the room and set a cup of hot tea in front of him. I watched as Jim slowly reached forward as if to feel where the cup was. When he found it, he moved it to a place in front of him that seemed to be familiar.

Then I looked at him, and just as I was about to speak, he said, "Stanley, you may have noticed something about me."

He paused for a moment. I think for dramatic effect.

Just Believe

"When I was about 28 years old, I lost my sight completely."

It was actually hard for me to tell. When he talked, he looked right at me. His head did not wander around like many blind people I have seen. He was very composed and comfortable with his surroundings.

"Mr. Stovall, I'll be honest. I did notice something, but it was really hard to tell."

He smiled. "First off, my name is Jim. My father is Mr. Stovall."

Kelly let out a little snort of a laugh. I had to laugh as well.

Then he asked, "Are you hungry? Let's order some food before we get started. Let me recommend The Stovall Special. It is a Caesar's salad with a nice piece of grilled salmon on top. You can't beat it."

"Sounds good to me," I said.

The waiter took our orders and promptly left the room.

I took out my journal and pen and got ready to write.

"So, I'm not really sure where to start. This is my first time doing this." I paused for a moment and then said, "What is it that you would like to teach me about The Message?"

"That's a good question, Stanley, and I'm glad you asked it. I guess it would have to start with my story. You see, I have not always been blind. I was born with sight just like you. Growing up, I was an athletic kid. I played Little League baseball and was pretty good at it. In fact, I was at a baseball game when I was seven years old when

Personal Initiative

I first noticed that my sight was failing me. I had a hard time hitting the baseball when it came across the plate. It was very frustrating, because I wanted to be good at it, but for some reason I was having difficulty seeing the ball as it came across the plate. Realizing that my baseball career wasn't going to happen, I moved my efforts over to football.

"In the South, football is a very big thing. I seemed to have a knack for it. I played all through junior and senior high school and graduated with a distinguished record. I am quite certain that my ability as a football star had a lot to do with my getting by academically.

"I wasn't sure what I wanted to do with my life, but all my friends were going to college, so it seemed to be the thing to do.

"I had received many offers of football scholarships to several universities, but I was still undecided. I remember filling out applications for a number of schools. One of the applications required a physical examination, including an eye test, in order to be admitted into college. I went through the motions of filling out the application, and I called our family's eye doctor in order to get the routine eye test as required.

"The doctor put drops in my eyes and shined a very bright light into them. After I read the chart as he instructed, I was preparing to leave, assuming the examination was over. About that time, a second doctor came in and repeated the same tests. Finally, a third doctor arrived and performed several additional procedures.

Just Believe

"I was starting to get a bit curious about the delay and all of the attention I was receiving from three separate doctors just to get my college application form signed.

"Finally, the three doctors took me down a long hall, and we sat down at a conference table. With very little preamble, they told me, 'We're not sure why, and we're not sure when, but we do know that someday you're going to be totally blind, and there's nothing we can do about it.' They told me that I had macular degeneration, which quite simply means that my eyes stopped making new cells. Eventually, over time, my sight would fade away until I was completely blind. In my case it took about ten years from the time of my diagnosis.

"When the doctor told me what was going on with my eyes, it was the most surreal moment I had ever experienced. I have thought of it many times since, and each of the details is in place as if it had just happened. It is one of those moments that is etched in your memory forever."

When he said that, I had to stop writing and look up at him.

"Believe me. I know exactly what you are talking about," I said.

He paused for a moment and then continued. "I was just, quite simply, in shock. I knew my eyesight was poor, but I had no idea that it would ever be any more than an inconvenience that I could ignore or bluff my way through."

He paused again, and I noticed I had not written anything yet, because I was so mesmerized by his story. Then I realized I needed to start writing. I opened the journal and started taking notes. He heard this, and he waited for me to get caught up. I could tell he was acutely aware of his surroundings. I stopped and looked back up at him. Then he continued.

"I attended college, and I will be honest with you. It was a rough time for me. My dreams of playing football professionally had faded away as my eyesight was fading away. I was dealing with depression, anger, sadness, and worst of all, self-pity.

"Fortunately, there was a messenger at the college. His name was Dr. Paul. He became my friend and mentor. He taught humanities at the school, which is the study of our development as a civilization. I realized that I had never before met anyone with that degree of passion about anything. He began to teach me the principles of The Message. Because of that, I have been able to share The Message with millions of people through my speaking engagements, books, and movies."

He stopped talking for a second.

"I'm getting ahead of myself."

"After I completed college, I began working as an investment broker and entrepreneur. I enjoyed a fair degree of success and was beginning to think that the doctor's diagnosis of my pending blindness had been just a bad dream.

"And then one morning, it happened. I woke up and realized my worst fear. My partial vision that I had learned to live with had left me completely, and I was totally blind. The thoughts and doubts and fears that came over me that morning would be almost impossible to describe to you. I wasn't sure what blind people did, because I had never met one. I was 29 years old, and I had no contingency plan for the rest of my life.

"Everything that I had wanted to do with my life had left me as my sight had left me. I felt as though I was completely alone in the world. I hid away in a 9x12-foot room in the back of my house. I gathered my radio, my telephone, and my tape recorder. This was my whole world at 29, and I really fully intended to never walk out of that room again.

"I would most likely still be there if it hadn't been for the instruction of Dr. Paul and the power of The Message he had given me.

"The other driving force was my love for people. I literally ached for people like you to talk to and share with. The process of getting out of that room was not easy or swift. It happened a little at a time, and it all began with a simple decision. I remember sitting there thinking that no matter what it was in the outside world that I was afraid of, it couldn't be worse than spending the rest of my life in this little 9x12-foot room. I was determined to get out of there.

"The first day, I walked 52 feet to the mailbox and returned to the house. From that humble beginning, my whole life changed because, as a blind person, I caught a new vision of who I could become.

"I remember talking with Dr. Paul, and he taught me the principle of personal initiative. Nothing was going to happen in my life unless I made it happen. I was determined to get out of that room and make a difference in the lives of all I would meet.

"Personal initiative is the driving force that allowed me to see beyond that small 9x12-foot world. If you will look back in history at any great success, it doesn't start with a confident, self-assured statement like, 'I know I'm going to make it' More often than not, it begins with a bit of fear and trembling and a statement such as 'I am willing to try and try again until we get there.'"

At that statement, the door opened to the room, and our waiter stepped in with three Stovall Specials. We took a moment to enjoy the meal. I must say it is one of the best salads I have ever had.

After a few bites, Jim jumped back into his story.

"Stanley, the purpose of our meeting today is for me to pass along one of the principles of The Message. You may have already deduced what the principle is, but I want to make sure you have a clear understanding of what personal initiative really is.

"Personal initiative is the dynamo that starts the faculty of imagination into action. It is the process that translates our definite purpose into physical or financial manifestation. If you aim for success above mediocrity, you will need to learn the power of personal initiative because your success is something you must achieve for yourself without someone telling you what to do or how to do it.

"Cyris H. Curtis, the owner of The Saturday Evening Post, said one time, 'There are two kinds of men who never amount to much: Those who cannot do as they are told, and those who can do nothing else.' What he meant by this is very clear. He was implying that those who amount to something worthwhile in life are those who move on their own personal initiative without being told what to do or why they should do it. The greatest successes in life are those who chose their own occupation and moved on their own personal initiative in achieving their purpose.

"You must understand, personal initiative must become a habit that will inspire you to move by your own responsibility. It will also influence you to carry through until you complete the task that you are undertaking."

I was writing as fast as I could, and Kelly cleared her throat. Jim stopped talking for a moment to let me catch up. I am assuming that this is a signal that they have developed over the years working together. I stopped writing and then he continued.

"You see, Stanley, it is important to understand that a big success is made up of a number of little circumstances, each of which could seem so small and insignificant within itself that you might pass it by without notice. Personal initiative is a quality that inspires people to form friendships and to make contacts with people that can be an aid to them in times of need.

"Let me share with you what has been shared with me about the important attributes of personal initiative so you can form the habit of personal initiative for yourself.

- "This person will have a definite major purpose in life and a plan to obtain it.

- "This person will seek out others who have like-minded goals and aspirations. This will allow each of them to achieve each others' goals.
- "This person will have the persistence and the will to win. This will help him along when the going is hard and he meets obstacles.
- "This person will make decisions promptly when he has obtained the necessary facts to base his decision. He will also change his mind slowly if he does at all.
- "This person will follow the habit of doing more than he is paid for. He will do this with a good and pleasing attitude.
- "This person accepts full responsibility for everything he undertakes and never passes the buck when things go wrong.
- "This person accepts criticism without resentment because he has learned that he can profit from it.
- "This person never expresses an opinion on anything unless he has thought the subject all the way through and is prepared to state how he has come by this opinion.
- "This person understands the importance of listening much and talking only when he has something of value to say, which may benefit himself or others.
- "This person will develop a sense of observation of small details and knows his job from the smallest detail to the greatest.

- "This person follows the habit of concentrating his full attention on one thing at a time.
- "This person's mental attitude is positive at all times when he is in communication with other people.
- "This person will give a clear and direct answer whenever he is asked a question. Even if he has to tell you he does not have an answer.
- "This person will never put off until tomorrow the things which should be done today. Because he knows that the habit of procrastination is at the top of the list for the causes of failure."

After firing off this list, he paused for a moment and took a sip of his tea. I wrote a couple more notes and then put down my pen. Jim set his cup down and then continued.

"You see, Stanley. I have been fortunate enough to be a recipient of The Message, but if I did not apply the principle of personal initiative to my life on a regular basis, I would still be sitting in that 9x12-foot room. Yes, it is scary. Yes, it will be hard work, but nothing that comes easy in life is worth having.

"Because I have applied the habit of personal initiative in my life, I have been able to do many great things. After I lost my eyesight, I realized that I would not be able to enjoy movies anymore since they are such a visual medium. I got the idea that if a movie could have a narrator describing what is being shown onscreen, blind or visually impaired people would be able to enjoy television or movies just as seeing people do. I decided that something had to be done about it, and I was the guy that was going to do it.

"With the help of my wife Crystal and my business partner Kathy Harper, we formed the Narrative Television Network. This company was formed to provide the service of narrating television shows and movies for the 13 million blind and visually impaired people in the United States today and millions more around the world. In doing this I have been able to meet hundreds of high profile people and share their stories with my audience. Through my talk show, I had the pleasure to interview many great people such as: Katharine Hepburn, Jimmy Stewart, Frank Sinatra, Michael Douglas, and many others.

"We were awarded an Emmy for our creation of the narrative process. I have spoken to over 4 million people over the past 15 years through my speaking engagements.

"A few years back, I wrote a book called *The Ultimate Gift*. It has been embraced by the public and has sold over 5 million copies. In 2005, it was made into a feature film staring the great James Garner. The movie has been shown around the world in many different languages and has sold many millions of copies. I write a weekly column that is in over 400 newspapers every week and read by over 3 million people. All of this is possible because I applied the principle of personal initiative.

"Please understand I am not telling you all of this to try to impress you or brag about my accomplishments. I tell this to prove to you that the principle and The Message work. This same amount of success is available to anyone and everyone who is willing to apply it in their lives. Stanley, you now have an opportunity to change the world around you with The Message. Please don't take it lightly."

And with that, he stopped. I looked over to Kelly who, I would guess, had heard this speech many times over, but I could tell she enjoyed every minute of it.

"Mr. Stovall, I mean Jim, thank you for your time and thank you for sharing this with me," I said.

"It is my distinct pleasure, Stanley. I am sure that we will meet again. In fact, I want you to meet a business partner of mine. He and I are doing what we can to change the world through movies. I think your story would make a great movie," he said.

I didn't know what to say to that. I just shook my head and said, "OK. That sounds great."

We finished our meal and then I dismissed myself. I had a lot to think about, and I needed to get writing. I had two principles of The Message now and I needed to get them on paper.

When I got up to leave the table, Jim looked over at me and said, "And Stanley, just remember, the best is yet to come."

That night, I told Lisa and the girls all about my meeting with Mr. Stovall. All of the things he had told me intrigued them. Josh got out a big colored piece of paper and put it up in their room. She wrote The Principles of The Message on the top of the paper and below it she started a list.

 1. Faith

2.   Personal Initiative.

She said, "When I grow up, I am going to be a messenger, too."

Later that evening, after we put the girls to bed, Lisa and I went for a walk. Cooper stayed home to watch the house.

"Lisa," I said, "I am seeing things differently now. My conversation with Mr. Stovall has opened my eyes to something that I never realized before."

"How so?" she asked.

"I used to think people got to where they were in life by luck or chance. I remember one guy in college whose dad was quite wealthy. We went to visit his family at their beach house in Florida on spring break. His father was telling me about a new business that he was launching and how it was going to yield him huge profits. I remember thinking to myself that he was lucky and that everything he touched seemed to turn to gold. Now I realize that, in a way, I was jealous of him. I took away any hard work or personal initiative that he may have had, and I equated his success to luck. After talking with Mr. Stovall, I now realize that he was successful because he decided to be successful, and he had the self-drive and self-motivation to make it happen."

She nodded her head in agreement.

I continued, "It changes everything for me. Now I realize that the future is mine to make. With just the first two principles of The Message, I believe that I could do anything. It just takes faith and personal initiative."

Just Believe

I looked at her and smiled as we continued our walk up the street. I so very much enjoyed our time together. She was still my angel.

Chapter Thirteen

Self-Discipline

"In reading the lives of great men, I found that the first victory they won was over themselves... self-discipline with all of them came first."
Harry S. Truman

The next day, I was at my desk working on the first two principles in the book when my phone rang. It felt good to be able to answer the phone and not expect to talk with a bill collector.

"Hello, this is Stan," I said when I picked up the phone.

"Mr. Walters?" came the reply on the other end.

"Yes," I said.

"Please hold for Mr. Trost."

Then I heard a click followed by hold music. I think it was an orchestrated version of *Too Much Heaven* by the Bee Gees. I hummed along until the song was interrupted with a voice.

"Hello Stan. This is Tracy Trost. I believe my friend and partner Jim Stovall told you about me."

Just Believe

"Oh, yes, yes. I had lunch with him yesterday," I said.

"Yes, I know. He told me all about it. I was wondering if you might have some time this afternoon to meet with me."

"This afternoon? Yeah, that should be fine," I replied.

"Great, I look forward to it. I'll have Carol email you the information. See you then."

"Bye," I said as I hung up the phone.

I wondered who this guy was and what he was going to share with me. I received the email and made arrangements for Miss Esther to pick up the girls from school and keep an eye on them until I got home. I grabbed my journal and was out the door.

I arrived at the offices of Trost Moving Pictures at 2 P.M. sharp as the email had instructed. A very pleasant young lady named Katy greeted me. She walked me through the offices and into a large room that had a Ping-Pong table in the middle of it. I was a little surprised to see a Ping-Pong table in a place of business. Katy noticed this and stopped for a second.

"Tracy and the rest of the guys here love to play. They really get into it and get pretty loud sometimes."

"Ah," I said. "Looks like fun."

"Do you play?" she asked.

"Well, actually yes. I played quite a bit in college, but it has been a long time."

She laughed a little. "Don't let Tracy know, or he'll challenge you to a game!"

We continued walking through the maze of offices through another large room that had a bunch of empty desks and cubicles. "What is this area?" I asked.

"Oh, this is the production room that we use to make movies. When we are shooting a movie, this becomes the central office for about three months. It is filled with all of the department heads and the production coordinator. It gets pretty busy when we are in full swing."

We continued on, and I could see an office that had a large window overlooking the production room. On the door was a nameplate that read

Tracy Trost *Lead Visionary.*

There were three people in the room talking. One was sitting behind the desk—I had to assume that this was Tracy. The other two sat in chairs in front of the desk. We stepped up to the door, and Tracy gave a wave to us to come in. They all stood as I entered.

"Hello Stanley, thanks for coming in," Tracy said. "We are just finishing up here. This is Jason, our producer. He actually holds many more titles than that, but we will just go with that one for now. And this is Joe; he is the producer of marketing and distribution. Don't ask me what it means. I just know he gets a lot done, and it sounds important."

We all chuckled at the comment and then Jason and Joe said their goodbyes, and I sat in one of the chairs in front of his desk.

His office was filled with trophies and awards from the different film festivals that his movies had won. The ledge by the window looking outside was filled with pictures of his family.

He leaned back in his chair and gave me a smile. "So, Stanley, what is the purpose of this meeting?"

I didn't know how to answer that. I was thinking that he wanted to meet with me.

He smiled at me again and said, "I'm just kidding! I know why you are here."

I laughed and said, "Good. You had me for a second."

He then leaned forward and said, "OK Stan. Can I call you Stan?"

"Yes, please," I replied.

He seemed satisfied with this answer.

"Stan, you have been selected to be given the 10 principles of The Message. I can't tell you how excited I am for you to do this. I remember when I first received The Message. It changed my life. I am not like most of the people you will meet on this very exciting journey. I did not have a tragic event, nor was I ready to give up on life. There are several messengers like me who were just average ordinary guys that were doing pretty well in life but knew there was something more. I was fortunate enough to grow up in a happy, well-balanced family. My parents were supportive and allowed me every opportunity to do just about anything I wanted to do.

"I got married at an early age to a beautiful, supportive woman. I have five wonderful children who are the joy of my life. I have been self-employed for most of my adult life and have been pretty successful at it. But even with all of this success, and all of the good things going on in my life, there was a part of me that was unfulfilled.

"You see, Stanley, I was doing all of the right things in life. I had a thriving business, and I was a good father, but there was something way deep down inside of me that wanted to get out, but I was afraid to go for it." He paused for a moment and thought. "Before I tell you what it was, I need to tell you how I discovered it.

"I own several companies. One of them is a marketing company. We provide direct mail and other marketing services for several Fortune 100 companies. A few years ago, I started a meeting with all of my employees—at that time about 11—called the book meeting. I am an avid reader which, I must say, started once I learned the principles of The Message. I like to read all different types of books about self-improvement and self-discipline.

"There was a man named Napoleon Hill who wrote one of my favorite books a long time ago. He wrote a book that was the result of over 25 years of study on the subject of success. He was able to interview over 500 different successful people of his time, and from that he wrote the book, *Think and Grow Rich*. I will be honest. There are two books that have been so profound in my life that, as a result of reading them, I made mental, physical, and spiritual changes to my life. The first is the *Bible*, and the second is *Think and Grow Rich*.

"You may be a little mislead by the title and think that it may be a get-rich-quick book. The opposite is true. It is a book that will teach you the habits you need to form that will bring you unlimited success in all areas of your life: mentally, spiritually, physically, and financially. By reading this book, I realized that the best thing I could ever do was help others to learn these truths. This was the inception of the book meetings.

"We hold the book meetings on Tuesdays. I bring in lunch, and we sit around our conference table. We eat together and talk about what is going on in each other's lives. I look forward to these meetings, because they are like getting together with family. We will then open our books to the chapter that we read that week and discuss how we can apply the truths of that particular chapter to our lives, within our business, and to our customers.

"During one particular meeting, we were discussing a chapter that was about dreams. The chapter asked the question, 'If you could do anything you wanted, be anyone you wanted to be, and money was not an issue, and failure was not an option, what would that one thing be? What would you do that would define you as a person?' When I asked that question, I looked around the room. Each of them was thinking about the question and each of them knew what their answer was. I went around the room and asked each person sitting at the table. One girl said she would be a photographer; one said she would be a massage therapist; and another said she would move to Colorado Springs.

"Then I asked them another question: 'What are you doing on a daily basis to get there?' We all know a journey takes planning. If I want to take a trip from Tulsa to California, I don't just say that I want to do it and then close my eyes and wake up in California. It takes planning.

I need to check dates, purchase a ticket, arrange transportation, and book lodging on the other end. I need to educate myself on the climate, culture, language, and practices of the people I will be seeing at my destination. It all takes planning. Life is very much like taking a trip; it takes planning. If there is a place that we want to be, we must plan to get there, or we will never arrive.

"My good friend Jim Stovall told me that, 'People will spend more time planning a three day vacation than they do planning their lives.' I have found this to be true. Many people thought as I did at one time. Life happens to you, and sometimes you are lucky and it turns out."

He paused for a second. Again, I was writing as fast as I could.

"I'll give you a second to catch up," he said with a smile. "Do you like coffee?" he asked.

"Yes, I do," I responded.

"Would you like some? I just got this great espresso machine. I can make you one of my famous lattes if you like," he said.

"Sure! That sounds great."

We walked down the hall past the Ping-Pong table.

"Do you play?" he asked me.

"I used to back in college," I replied.

"We will have to get a game in before you go. It is a great stress reliever," he said.

We continued down a long hall and entered a kitchen area. He walked over to the espresso machine and turned it on. It started gurgling as he continued to talk.

"So, back to my story. When I asked everyone about what they were doing to reach their dreams, none of them had an answer. I think that is how most people live their lives. To be honest, I was doing the same thing at the time. After I had asked them about what they were doing on a daily basis to realize their dreams, one of the girls spoke up and looked me straight in the eyes and asked, 'Tracy, what would you do if you could do anything you wanted?'

"I knew the answer right away. I think most of them thought that I was going to say running a business. Don't get me wrong. I did love my work, and I loved the people I worked with, but it was not my dream or my passion. No, my dream was to be a director. Ever since I was a young man I have always wanted to direct movies. So I told her, if I could do anything I wanted to, I would be a director.

"Then she looked at me with a smile. 'Well then, what are you doing on a daily basis to get there?'

"Ouch! I was hit with my own words. I really didn't have an answer for her. You know what it's like. You get married, have kids, buy a house. You have mouths and a mortgage to feed. Your focus goes to making money, not following your dreams. I'll be honest with you, I did not expect those questions to come back at me. The experience really got me thinking.

"I went home that night and told my wife about the meeting. She looked at me and said, 'Yes, Tracy, when *are* you going to do that? You have always said that *one day* you would be a director. You told me that when we first met. That is over 22 years ago. You need to do it.'"

He stopped talking for a moment and concentrated on steaming the milk for my coffee. I could tell he was taking great delight in making me his special cup. He turned off the steamer and placed the cup below the espresso steamer and hit the button. The machine made a clicking noise and dark fragrant coffee started coming out of the nozzle into the cup.

"Ah, can you smell that? It's good stuff," he said.

I could tell he had a genuine appreciation for the brown liquid.

Once the coffee was brewed, he added the milk and took a spoon and stirred it. Then he handed it to me. He continued talking as he made himself a cup.

"You see, Stan, this was a turning point for me in my life. I could face my fears, or I could continue what I was doing and never fulfill my dream of being a director. To do this, I knew it was going to take great discipline. Making a move is an arduous process that takes great discipline to complete."

He finished making his cup of coffee and sat next to me at the counter.

"This is the principle of The Message that I want to share with you: self-discipline."

"Self-discipline, as I am going to explain it to you, is not only in reference to the mastery of negative habits, which stand in the way of your success, but will apply to the creation of positive habits. I am going to give you a list of habits that, if applied to anyone's life in conjunction with the other principles of The Message, will help a person achieve any goal they set before themselves.

- "LEARN THE HABIT OF THINKING BEFORE SPEAKING.

  "It is important to think of what you want to say and be sure that it will be a benefit to yourself and those around you. A loose tongue can become your greatest liability.

- "LEARN THE HABIT OF PATIENCE WITH OTHER PEOPLE.

  "This is an important one. Learning to control the tendency to strike back at someone who may have wronged you is vital. You must remember that anything you do to or for another, you do to or for yourself. Your every thought or every act that benefits or injures another person comes back to you in the same manner, greatly multiplied. So if you must slander another person do not speak it. Write it. Write it in the sands near the water's edge, and then move away from it until the tides have washed it away for good.

- "LEARN THE HABIT OF CONTROLLING YOUR EMOTIONS.

  "Most importantly you need to learn to control your emotions of love, hate, fear, and sex. These are the big four that need constant evaluation. They can make you or break you depending on what you allow them to do or become in your life.

Self-Discipline

- "DEVELOP THE HABIT OF CONTROLLING YOUR MENTAL ATTITUDE.

  "The Lack of a good mental attitude will eventually drive away friends, destroy opportunities, bring on physical and mental illness, develop into stomach ulcers, and make peace of mind impossible. Be sure to fill your mind with positive thoughts that will breed other positive thoughts.

- "DEVELOP CONTROL OVER THE EMOTION OF SEX.

  "I mentioned this emotion earlier, but it is so important that I need to address it again. Failure to exercise self-discipline over this emotion probably heads the list of all the causes of personal failure. The emotion of sex is the most powerful of all emotions, and it is nature's great creative instrument in which all living species are perpetuated. The proper means of self-discipline of the emotion of sex is transmutation, or learning to redirect the energy of that emotion to another resource. The control and direction of the emotion of sex toward the obtainment of worthy purpose, such as the fulfillment of your dream, is the key to overcoming the emotion of sex. The great leaders in life have learned the art of transmutation through the proper system of self-discipline. This is something that every person deals with at one time or another. Overcoming the power of this emotion is a big step toward fulfillment of your personal dreams or goals.

- "DEVELOP A SYSTEM OF PROPER DIETING AND FASTING.

   "Seek out information on the proper diet and lifestyle in the consumption of food. If you can learn to discipline yourself when it comes to food, you can overcome any other force in life. Good health and regular exercise are key to achiving your goals in life.

- "DEVELOP DISCIPLINE IN THE AREA OF FAITH AND SPIRITUALITY.

   "Our country, which to date has proven to be the best form of civilization, is made up of people of varying beliefs. To be happy and prosperous in this country, we must learn to live and let live and to give others the privileges we ask and demand for ourselves. This often calls for strict discipline over our own spirituality. You need to get an understanding of the creative power that has been given to you by your creator so that you may live in the knowledge and peace that will propel you in your definite major purpose.

- "LEARN THE HABIT OF TAKING CONTROL OF YOUR OWN MIND.

   "You cannot take possession of your own mind or direct it to definite ends without a practical system. There is a system that is simple, but if used, it will create profound results to the user. It does not call for you to be a genius, and it does not call for a large amount of formal education. It calls only for the will to take possession of one's own mind and a definite purpose to which the mind is to be directed. Practice directing your mind to specific thoughts and purposes on a regular basis. Take possession of the thought patterns that present themselves in your mind and steer them on the path that will lead you to success in obtaining your definite major purpose."

By this time, Tracy had finished drinking his coffee and took his cup to the sink.

"You see, Stan, it is simple, and at the same time very profound. Through self-discipline, you a can do anything you want." He pointed to his forehead. "It allows you to conquer this thing up here in between our ears. All of our struggles, doubts, fears, and everything that holds us back in life are nothing more than a thought. Through the principle of self-discipline, you can learn to control the effect that those thoughts can or cannot have in your life.

"Through the principle of self-discipline, I was able to write my first script. I will be honest with you. It was not easy. It didn't just flow out of me. I had to work at it for a long time. There was a period of time for about 6 months that I actually gave up. I kept hearing my inner voice tell me that it was too hard and not good enough. You know that voice, don't you?" he asked me.

I nodded my head in agreement.

"The truth is, we all do. We all have an inner voice that is always talking to us. You need to realize that you have the power to direct that inner voice and to train it to encourage you instead of discourage you. Through self-discipline, you can train your inner voice to feed you positive thoughts. It takes time and consistent discipline, but it can be done. I had to conquer my fear and my inner voice until I started working on the script again.

"Over about a year, I wrote ten different versions of my script until I felt like I had something that would be ready to shoot. Then I sent it to a script consultant who ripped it apart and made me rewrite it again. This was all training for me, and it would not have happened if I were not able to silence that inner voice of fear in my mind. By using the principle of self-discipline, I filled my mind with thoughts of faith and perseverance."

By this time, we had worked our way back to his office.

"That first script turned into a movie—*Find Me*, which has won awards in several different film festivals. There are some of them right there."

He pointed to some of the awards on his wall.

"Jim tells me your story would make a good movie," he said.

I wasn't sure what to think: my *story*. It sounded funny. I guess the idea of getting a lamp, and then meeting a messenger, and getting three wishes that I didn't need was a little out there, but it might make a good movie.

"Ah, yeah. I guess so. I am working on writing a book right now."

"I would love to read it when you are done, if that is OK with you," he said.

"Sure. I'll make sure to get you a copy."

He nodded.

On our way out, we stopped and played a couple games of Ping-Pong. I won one of the games, though I have the feeling he let me win.

When I got home, Lisa and the girls had dinner ready. They were excited to hear about my meeting and were full of questions. They wanted to know about the newest principle of self-discipline. Josh went in her room and brought her poster to the table. She took out her marker and added the third principle to her list.

The Principles of The Message

1. Faith
2. Personal Initiative
3. Self-Discipline

Chapter Fourteen

Go the Extra Mile

"I find the harder I work, the more luck I seem to have!"

Thomas Jefferson

The next morning, I got up early so I could work on my book. I was at my desk when Lisa and the girls got up to go to school. I took a short break to say my good-byes.

"I'll be out front to pick you up when you get done with school," I told them.

"OK Daddy," they both said in unison.

Daddy! I remember that not too long before I never thought I would be called that again. I was so very blessed to have these girls in my life.

After they left, Cooper walked up to me and gave me his little groan and head turn. That was my cue. It was time for his walk. I was happy to do it. Walking with him always allows me time to clear my head and think about what I need to write.

Just Believe

On this particular day, I had a lot to think about. Tracy had made a comment that got me thinking about something I had not thought about in a long time. One of the points to the principle of self-discipline was in the area of faith and spirituality. To be honest, I was never much of a churchgoer, but the more I was learning about these principles, the more I could see different Scriptures being integrated in the different points of The Message. I began to wonder: What really was this Message? What is its origin?

I was totally intrigued by this whole experience. Charles also said something that was sticking with me. The thought that living for others could become a lifestyle that would give me everything I could ever wish for. It almost seemed opposite to everything that I had learned growing up. I can attest to the validity of it. I experienced it with Josh. When I was able to take my eyes off of my issues and focus on helping her, I was set free. I can still remember that day when I gave her Eddy's glove. It was the most freeing experience I had ever had. It brought my heartbeat back to me and changed the way I will see life for the rest of my existence.

I was so deep in thought that I did not realize that we had reached the park. Cooper sat down waiting for me to unhook him from his leash. I snapped back to reality and let him run. I walked up the hill, and I could see a man sitting and reading a paper. I started walking straight for him, and as I did, I could see that it was Sam.

He put down the paper and motioned for me to come sit by him. When I reached him, he greeted me with a big grin.

"Good morning, Stanley," he said.

I was really glad to see him.

"Good morning, Sam!" I replied.

We sat in silence and watched Cooper chase the squirrels for a moment, and then he spoke.

"How is it going with your training?"

"Good, good, I think. There is a lot of information to digest," I replied.

"Yes, it may seem like a lot. But trust me, once you study them and commit them to your heart, they will become a way of life for you. The Message will become second nature to you, replacing your old way of thinking. My favorite book says that if you want to transform your life, you must do it by renewing your mind. That is all you are doing."

I thought about what he said, and it made sense. One thing that I had learned from Charles and the *just believe* or *faith* part of The Message is that it all starts with being willing to believe. That happens in your mind.

We sat there for a few more moments and then I said, "Sam, how did you learn about The Message?"

He sat back in the bench and ran his fingers through his hair as if he was turning on his memory to tell the story.

"Well, Stanley, it was a long time ago. I was a much younger man."

He paused again thinking of where to start his story.

Just Believe

"I was born during a time when the country was in a bad place. Jobs were scarce, and my family was very poor. When I was eight years old, my mother died. Two years later, my father married another woman.

"When I was 13, I started writing. I think, for me, it was a way of escape. I enjoyed creating characters in my head and taking them through adventures. As I got older, I started writing stories about people of the day. I liked telling stories that had a purpose to them and left people with a message. I ended up going to college and eventually became an attorney. I still kept my writing up. As a matter of fact, I actually paid my college bill by being a journalist for various newspapers.

"One day, I met with my editor, and he gave me an assignment to write a series of success stories of famous men. Little did I know, that assignment would lead me to discovering The Message. I was fortunate enough to meet some very influential people who the world would say were the most successful people of their time.

"There was one in particular named Andrew who was a great industrialist and had more wealth than most small countries. He was intrigued by the human mind and the power of the subconscious. I wrote a success article about him, and he liked my writing. He asked for a meeting one day to discuss an idea that he had. I went to meet with him, and he laid a plan out before me.

"He said, 'I want you to do a study of the most successful people in the world. I am not sure how long this will take, but I am willing to fund it for as long as it takes. I want to discover the formula to success.'

"Well, I don't have to tell you that I was hooked. To meet the world's most successful people, and to have the assignment to discover what elements are in place that allowed all of them to be the success that they are, was an honor. I started working on it right away.

"With Andrew's help, I had meetings set up for the next two years. I thought that I would be able to do these interviews and then write the study within a couple of years. Little did I know that my quest would consume me and become my life."

He stopped and looked at me. He could tell I was a little fidgety. I realized that this meeting with Sam was going to be another principle of The Message. I did not have anything to write with, and I was trying to think of a way to remember all he was going to tell me. Sam smiled at me for a second and reached over to his left side.

"Here, Stanley," he said as he handed me my journal and pen. "You might want this," he said with a smile.

"Thanks," is all I could say. "I must remember to take my journal with me everywhere I go."

"Stanley, I want to share another principle of The Message with you. It is the principle of going the extra mile. I want to tell you all I know about this important principle in the hopes that you will be able to apply it to your life and understand how important it is. This is the one principle that one must follow if they expect to write their own price tag and to be sure of getting it.

"Let me give this principle to you in a form that you will easily recall. I call it the **QQMA** formula, which means the **Quality** of service you render plus the **Quantity** of service you render plus the **Mental Attitude** in which you render the service. This determines the space you occupy in your chosen profession and the compensation you will get for your services.

"If you were to examine all of the people that are successful, you would find that they follow the QQMA formula. They may be doing this unconsciously. I want to give you an advantage over those who may follow this formula unconsciously. I want to show you how to make use of it deliberately with purpose and forethought. In doing this, you will be able to make this principle pay off in a big way and do it quickly.

"I want to give you a list of the benefits of following the principle of going the extra mile.

- "Going the Extra Mile will help you gain the attention of other people who can and will provide you with opportunities to promote yourself into a better circumstance.

- "Going the Extra Mile will activate the natural law of increasing returns through which the service you provide will bring back greater than average return to you.

- "Going the Extra Mile will make you indispensable in your chosen occupation or calling; therefore, it will place you in a position to write your own paycheck.

- "Going the Extra Mile will help you to excel in your line of work because you will endeavor to do a better job than you did in the past.

Go the Extra Mile

- "Going the Extra Mile will give you preferential treatment when you are in the position of working for a salary or wages—especially when work is slow and others are laid off.
- "Going the Extra Mile will help you to benefit because the others around you will not be going the first mile, let alone the second.
- "Going the Extra Mile will cause you to do your very best in all of your efforts, and doing it with a pleasing mental attitude will improve your personality and will draw other people to you.
- "Going the Extra Mile will help you in developing your imagination because you will be continually seeking new and better ways of doing things.
- "Going the Extra Mile will inspire you to move on your own personal initiative instead of waiting to be told what to do. This is key to personal achievement. Many people are standing by, waiting for opportunity to come when they need to step out and make things happen on their own.
- "Going the Extra Mile will influence people to respect you and your integrity, and it will inspire others to go out of their way to work with you.
- "Going the Extra Mile helps you to develop definiteness of purpose, which is the starting point of all personal success.
- "Going the Extra Mile provides you with the one and only excuse for asking for and receiving higher pay. Obviously, if you are doing no more than you are being paid for, then you are already

receiving pay for which you are entitled, and you have no reason for asking for more money or a promotion.

- "Going the Extra Mile trains your mind to maintain a mastermind alliance with others. You will learn more about this in the future."

He paused for a moment to let me catch up on my notes. This was all great information.

"You know something, Sam?" I said. "If people could follow just one of the principles, it would change their lives."

"That is a true statement if I ever heard one," he replied. "When Andrew gave me the task to study personal success, I had no idea what it would entail. I thought two years would be a long time to write this study. I tell you now that, in total, I worked on this project for 25 years. I had the privilege of interviewing over 500 people who were the world's most successful people. It was my great honor. But I must be honest with you. If I did not go the extra mile on this and every project that I worked on, I would have never been afforded the opportunity. You must realize that the principle of going the extra mile develops greater self-reliance and gives you more courage to move ahead without the fear of criticism from others. It also helps you to master the destructive habit of procrastination—the one habit that heads the list of causes of failure.

"I can tell you frankly that I have never received a major break during my entire life that did not come from having applied the principle of going the extra mile. There have been times when I have heard others complain that their positions are such that they are not permitted to go the extra mile, and my counsel to these people is always the same: Change positions and market your services where it pays to go the extra mile.

"You now have in your possession the fourth principle of The Message. In order that you may test the truth of this principle, I am going to offer you a suggestion that may bring you such success that you may not need to learn any of the other principles of The Message.

"My suggestion is this:

"First, start tomorrow in whatever project you are working on to give some form of useful service to someone near you which you are not expected to give and for which you neither expect nor ask for payment.

"Second, give this service with a pleasing mental attitude which will clearly show that you enjoy doing it.

"Third, follow this practice seven days in a row and then notice what a changed atmosphere you will enjoy in your association with those around you.

"This does not have to be something that is only done in the workplace. This principle applies to all areas of life, especially in the home and in marriage.

"When you follow these instructions, don't let anyone know what you are up to. Be sure to do it in the most natural way possible to you. I will bet you that by the end of the seventh day you will find yourself so much happier and so much better liked by those around you that you will never desire to give up this habit."

With that, Sam leaned back in the bench and let out a sigh. His work was done here.

Cooper came up to us, and Sam gave him a pat on the head. It was time for me to go.

"Thank you, Sam, for all of your help and instruction."

"It is my pleasure, Stanley. I look forward to our next meeting," he said.

I said good-bye and put the leash back on Cooper. As I walked away, Sam picked up the paper and continued reading just as he was when I had arrived.

Since I had an early start on the day, and had my principle meeting for the day, I decided to surprise Lisa and meet her for lunch at work. I pulled up to the gym, and I could see her through the glass working with a client. When she saw me, she excused herself and came over to me as I entered the building. She had a huge smile on her face.

"What are you doing here?"

"Oh, I thought I would take you out to lunch," I replied.

"OK, give me five minutes, and I'll be right out," she said and walked back over to her client and finished up.

We went to lunch at one of our favorite local places: Aguila O Sol. Aguila O Sol loosely translates to *eagle or sun*.

On one of the Mexican coins, one side has an eagle, while the other has a sun. In North America we say heads or tails when we have a coin toss. In Mexico, it is eagle or sun. I love this place because it is an authentic Mexican place owned by a very sweet lady named Gabriella. We love to eat there because the food is great, and Gabby makes you feel like family. I guess you would say she "goes the extra mile."

As we ate, I told Lisa all about my conversation with Sam and about the new principle.

"If you don't mind," she said, "I am going to write down that exercise and have my people do that with our customers. I think it is exactly what we need."

I was glad to be of service. We enjoyed our meal and our time together. I took her back to the gym and then went to pick up the girls from school. I got there a little early, so I took out my journal and went over my notes. I couldn't wait to start writing when I got home.

Josh and Rachael jumped in the car, and Josh saw that I was looking through my journal.

"Did you meet someone new today?" she asked.

"No, actually I met with Sam again. He told me the next principle."

"I wish I could meet him," she said.

I guess I never realized that no one else had seen Sam yet.

"What is it?" she inquired.

"Here," I handed her my journal. "You can read it to us on the way home."

She dug right into it. I am amazed at how young children can grasp truth when it is presented to them. Even Rachael enjoyed hearing my notes.

That night, as I tucked the girls in bed, I did something that I had never done before.

"Do you girls mind if I say a prayer before you go to sleep?" I asked them.

"Let's do it!" Rachael responded.

"We used to pray with Miss Esther every night," Josh said.

I didn't really know where to start, and I think Josh could tell, so she jumped in.

"Dear God, I thank You for teaching my daddy the principles of The Message. I pray that he will help You change the world. Amen."

I opened my eyes for a second and then she continued. "Oh yea and please let me hit a home run this year. Amen."

Rachael and I followed suit.

"Amen."

We chuckled a little and then I kissed the girls goodnight. As I was reaching over to turn the light off, I could see Josh's poster.

The Principles Of The Message
1. Faith
2. Personal Initiative
3. Self-Discipline
4. Go The Extra Mile

Chapter Fifteen

Enthusiasm

"A man can succeed at almost anything for which he has unlimited enthusiasm."

Charles Schwab

The next morning, I was back at my post working on the book. Lisa and the girls were gone carrying out their day.

Cooper had waited as long as he could for me to take him on our walk. He came in the room with his leash in his mouth and gave me his stare down. I swear that dog could set a world record for staring. I got the hint.

"Come on, Coop ol' boy! Let's do it."

His tail started wagging, and we were off. I took the leash from him and attached it to his collar as we left the office and took a right turn for the front door. As we turned the corner, I noticed an envelope at the base of the front door. I picked it up and turned it over. *Stanley* was written on it in ink. I broke the seal and opened it up.

Inside there was only a business card with the name Paula Marshall, with the Bama Pie Corporation. There was the usual information such as address and phone number. I turned the card over, and there was a cell phone number handwritten on the backside, and underneath it 10:00 A.M. was written.

I looked down at Cooper who was looking at me impatiently, and then I looked at the clock. It was 9:00 A.M. I had time to take Cooper on his walk and then come back and make the call.

I got back to the house at five minutes 'til 10:00 and sat at my desk. Sitting there watching the clock tick away was torture. Those five minutes seemed like an hour. The clock finally hit 10:00 A.M., and I dialed the number. It rang twice, and then I heard a voice on the other side.

"This is Paula."

I didn't know what to say really, so I stammered on my words at first.

"Ah, yes, I got your card at my house today and it had a numb…."

"Yes, Stanley, Charles asked me if it was OK to give it to you," she said.

"Oh, OK well um, I'm not sure where to go from here," I said.

"How about you and I have a visit. Can you come by this morning before lunch? Say 11:30 A.M."

"Yes. That would be great," I said.

"OK. I'll see you then. The address is on the card. Good-bye."

And with that she hung up. I could tell she was a very busy person, and she moved from one thing to the next.

Enthusiasm

I didn't know who she was or what the Bama Pie Company was for that matter, so I took a little time to do some research. It turns out the company has been around since the 1920s. It is the largest producer of biscuits and pies to some of the worlds largest restaurant chains. Paula has been the CEO of this corporation since 1984.

When I arrived at the offices, I was taken aback by how friendly the woman at the front desk was. She greeted me with a big smile as I walked in the front door.

"How can I help you, sir?" she asked me.

"I'm here to meet with Ms. Marshall. I have an 11:30 appointment," I said with as much importance as I could summon.

"Oh yes. You must be Mr. Walters. Come right in. Paula is expecting you."

Paula? She calls the CEO of the company by her first name?

The door to the outer office opened, and another friendly lady greeted me.

"Hi, I am Rosemary. I'll take you to Paula. Just follow me," she said as she turned and started walking.

We walked down a couple of different halls and around several corners. The building was very large. You could hear the faint hum of machinery in the background. I spoke up, "Rosemary, I hope you don't mind if I ask you a question."

"No. Go right ahead," she said.

"I noticed that both you and the secretary called Ms. Marshall by her first name."

"Yes," she replied.

"Well, I find that kind of odd, being that she is the CEO of a very large organization," I said, a little puzzled.

"Oh, dear, you must understand Paula. She wouldn't have it any other way. She has developed a very family-oriented, exciting atmosphere here," Rosemary explained.

We arrived at our final destination, which turned out to be a conference room. Rosemary stopped at the doorway and motioned for me to go in.

"I'll let Paula know that you are here. Please have a seat."

"Thanks," I said as I entered the room.

"Can I get you any coffee or tea perhaps?" she asked before leaving.

"I'm fine," I said as I found a seat.

The conference room was very nice. It was painted all in white. The back wall had four tiers of shelving on it, and every tier held at least 50 different awards given to Paula and Bama Pie. I could see by the list of clientele that they provided product to the number one food chains in the markets. It was all very impressive. I was reading the different awards when Paula walked in the room.

"Hello Stanley, I am so glad you could make it."

I turned and greeted her: "Thank you, Ms. Marshall. It is an honor."

"Please, call me Paula," she said. She motioned for me to sit.

"I hope you don't mind, but I did some research on you before I came. I must say you and your organization are very impressive. I can see why Charles wanted me to meet you," I commented.

"Don't let all the press fool you. I am a normal, everyday person just like you. Fortunately for me, I was able to learn The Message at an early age. You see, Stanley, I have been on both sides of the coin when it comes to success. I have been as poor as the poorest people, and I have been as wealthy as some of the wealthiest people in the world. I can guarantee you this: Wealth does not bring happiness. It is a tool that, if used correctly, can bring great joy to many; if it is used incorrectly, however, it can become an evil taskmaster.

"I pretty much had a normal childhood, and, just like any other kid growing up in America, I went to high school and was getting ready to go to college when I had an unexpected event happen in my life. I got pregnant. This was very unexpected, and at the same time, one of the biggest blessings of my life. I left college, had my daughter, and came to work at Bama Pie on the assembly line. That is how I got my start at Bama.

"Even though I was in the family—you see my grandmother started Bama in 1920—I was not given the keys to the company. I had to work my way up. I didn't realize it at the time, but my sense of enthusiasm—and my good attitude of gratitude—opened doors for me as I applied myself to my job. Over the next 14 years, I worked my way to the position that I am in now.

"We have thousands of employees throughout the world. The amazing thing is that even though we are a large corporation, as the CEO, I have been able to keep the family atmosphere within the organization. I have mainly been able to do this through enthusiasm. Whenever I go out and meet with my team members, I try to bring with me a sense of excitement or enthusiasm."

"I noticed that the ladies here in the office call you by your first name. I have to be honest, that surprised me," I said.

She thought about that for a moment. "I guess in most cases that might seem a little too familiar, but we are family here. I wouldn't have it any other way."

Then she continued, "I have heard it said that knowledge is power. I would say that is a half-truth. Knowledge becomes power only when it is put into action for the obtainment of a definite objective. Enthusiasm is one of the more powerful means in which we can put into action our education, experience, and knowledge. When you talk without enthusiasm, you are usually ineffective. You know what I mean. Have you ever listened to a speaker who was not enthusiastic about his message? He can put you to sleep.

"Through my studies, I have learned a lot about enthusiasm and I would like to break down for you why it has such a powerful impact on those who come in contact with it. Your brain, and every other person's brain, is both a broadcasting and receiving station that sends out thought vibrations and also picks up those sent out by other people. When you turn on your enthusiasm, you step up the vibrations of thoughts that come from your brain so that they reach and affect other people more quickly. You can send out thoughts that have been so stepped up with enthusiasm that they will reach and influence other people with whom you have contact. This is a fact that has been known to physiologists for years now. You might be interested to know that most of the top salesmen use this technique. Some know they are using it, and others do it by instinct.

"I am sure that you have noticed in your life, Stanley, that enthusiasm is very contagious. It engages the attention of those who come under its influence and causes them to respond in a similar manner.

"I read a quote one time by Andrew Carnegie. He said, 'If you turn loose one man who thought in terms of intense enthusiasm in an industrial plant employing thousands of people, this man's enthusiasm would very quickly reach and influence every person in the plant.' There is something you must understand about that statement that most overlook. It does not make any difference whether the enthusiasm was negative or positive, constructive or destructive.

"When I look to promote one of my employees, one of the biggest things I look for is a person's capacity to express themselves with intense enthusiasm. Enthusiasm is one of the most important traits necessary for leadership.

"Let me give you an outline of what a good leader should do to be successful in their business or personal life. This is especially true for those who are in the profession of sales. One thing you must consider. Even if you are not a professional salesperson, at one time or another you are selling yourself and who you are to those around you. These tips will help you if you take them to heart and make them part of your persona.

"When you meet another person, turn on your enthusiasm, and when you do, modulate your voice so that you definitely make the other person feel you are happy to communicate with him.

"When you shake his hand, grip it firmly, and give it a good firm squeeze each time you talk to him.

"When you begin the conversation, be sure that you direct it to a subject that is of interest to the other person.

"Follow through by eagerly asking questions that keep the attention focused on the other person. Then when you are ready to have the other person hear what you have to say about yourself, or your business, he will be prepared to listen attentively.

"I have a friend who is a doctor. He has had a general practice in town for over 20 years. He told me one time that the best piece of medicine that he carries is his enthusiasm. He believes it has more to do with bringing about a cure than all the medicine he can prescribe.

"The principle of enthusiasm is a power that, once released, has been credited with helping bring about a cure for the sick and is more effective than most of the medical procedures prescribed. Enthusiasm not only influences those who carry it, but it also influences and benefits those who follow the habit of expressing it in their thoughts and deeds. Enthusiasm is an expression of a positive mental attitude, and it has long been known to doctors that a positive mental attitude stands high on the list of influences that give one sound health."

Enthusiasm

She paused for a moment to let me take all of this in. It seemed that her countenance changed a little, and she got a more serious look on her face.

"Stanley, there is one more thing that I would like to share with you that I have learned about the principle of enthusiasm. I believe that this is the most important lesson that I can share with you about this principle. It has been my experience that prayer expressed with enthusiasm brings much quicker and more satisfactory results. I would challenge you to try this for yourself so you know that I am not just making it up. I started doing this myself many years ago, and I have found that if you apply the practice that I am about to share with you, you can achieve any goal you may set in place.

"A good place to start in learning how to express yourself with enthusiasm is to form the habit of reading out loud for at least ten minutes daily. Put all the enthusiasm that you have into your reading. I know this sounds strange, but you will be surprised that in a very short time this will help you in speaking with enthusiasm in your ordinary conversations. I would suggest also that you adopt the habit of practicing enthusiasm in your conversations with your family and your business associates. You will find that in doing this, you will become more popular with your friends and those who are close to you.

"You will be able to enjoy the benefits of enthusiasm if you will be self-disciplined enough to develop the technique so that you can do it in a natural, unaffected tone of voice.

"The first step is what I just suggested: Read for ten minutes daily as a means of acquiring the habit of enthusiasm. I recommend that you write down a list of ten subjects, things, or circumstances in which you have interest. Use this list for your practice purposes. You will find that it will become second nature to you to read with a tone of enthusiasm in connection with the things that you like or are interested in."

She paused for a second, as if she were recalling a past memory. I stopped writing and looked up at her.

"Stanley, do you remember what it was like when you were first in love?"

"Yeah, I guess so," I said.

"Do you think that you were enthusiastic when you were in pursuit of her?" she asked.

"Oh, yes. I did not have to try to create any kind of enthusiasm. It was there," I said.

"Exactly. Enthusiasm is always easily expressed when you are inspired by the desire for something that you are interested in. When there is no motive, there will most likely be no enthusiasm. Don't forget that the three basic motives that rule the world are the emotion of love, the emotion of sex, and finally the desire for financial gain. It has been said that the combination of all three of these motives can convert a mediocre person into a genius." She smiled at me and then said, "I'll let you think about that one for a moment."

She then leaned forward in her chair and cleared her throat. I could tell that she had finished sharing the principle of enthusiasm with me.

Enthusiasm

"Stanley," she said, "I can only request one thing from you or anyone that I share the principles of The Message with. I would ask that you try to apply the principle of enthusiasm to everything you do in your daily life. I am sure you will not regret it."

At that, she stood up and put out her hand. I quickly grabbed all of my things, shook her hand, and then I was on my way.

"Thank you so much for your time." As I shook her hand, I was sure to give it a good squeeze. She noticed this.

"Nice, Stanley. You were listening," she complimented.

After my meeting with Paula, I ran some errands and then picked the girls up from school. Josh jumped in the front seat and saw my journal sitting on the seat.

"Who did you meet today?" she asked with all kinds of enthusiasm.

I paused for a second as I considered what just happened. Most of the kids that I have seen are enthusiastic. They are excited about life and all the things going on around them. I could remember back to when I was a kid. I was enthusiastic about everything. What happens as we get older? Why do we lose that sense of enthusiasm? I vowed to myself at that moment to regain my sense of enthusiasm and to allow myself to be excited about things again.

Then Josh said, "Ahem! Earth to Dad."

"Oh, sorry honey. I met a very nice lady name Paula. She taught me the principle of enthusiasm. It was very enlightening."

Just Believe

Rachael asked, "What's enthusiasm?"

Josh answered for me. "It's when you are excited about life and happy to be alive."

"Yeah. What she said," I added.

"OK then, I'm enthusiasm," chimed Rachael.

"Enthusiastic," Josh corrected her. We all had a good chuckle at her comment.

That night as I kissed the girls goodnight, I looked at Josh's Poster.

The Principles of The Message

1. Faith
2. Personal Initiative
3. Self-Discipline
4. Go The Extra Mile
5. Enthusiasm

Chapter Sixteen

Overcoming Adversity

"All the adversity I've had in my life, all my troubles and obstacles, have strengthened me.... You may not realize it when it happens, but a kick in the teeth may be the best thing in the world for you."

Walt Disney

The next day was Saturday. The girls and I went over to the ball field right after breakfast to get set up for practice. It was a beautiful spring morning. There was a hint of dew on the grass, and the air was sweet and cool. The sun was getting higher in the sky and warming things up. Josh and I were throwing the ball to warm up and Rachael and Cooper were sitting on the bleachers. Rachael was reading one of her books.

I was taking in the moment, and I realized that my life was so rich with blessings. Almost three years earlier, right after I lost Eddy, I could have never imagined being this happy again. I realized that it was OK to move on in life. Not that I would ever forget him, but that it was OK to live even though he was not with me anymore.

The rest of the team began showing up, and I started practice. I had them running drills, and we were focusing on infield play. I was batting balls to the third base player and the shortstop to give them practice stopping the ball when I noticed Sam walking along the outfield fence.

"Great!" I said out loud.

I didn't bring my journal to practice. I have to remember to keep it with me at all times. I never know where these guys will turn up. He stopped at the right field bleachers and sat down. Cooper saw him and trotted over to him for a pet.

I called Jason to take over on batting. Before I left, I bent over so I could see Jason face to face.

"Hey buddy," I said.

"Yeah, coach?" he replied.

"Take a look at the bleacher behind right field."

He turned his head toward right field.

"Yeah?" he said.

"Do you see anyone sitting on the bleachers?" I asked.

He looked a little harder and then he looked back at me.

"I see Cooper sitting on the bleachers; that's all."

I looked over and could distinctly see Sam sitting there. He noticed me looking at him and waved.

"OK, buddy. Thanks!" I said.

"You OK, coach?" he asked.

"Yeah, yeah. I'm fine. Do me a favor and work on some infield grounders. OK?" I said.

"Sure thing, coach."

Jason took the bat and started hitting some balls to the shortstop. I stood there for a while before I started walking toward the back bleachers. I didn't want Jason to think I was going crazy.

I walked up to Sam and sat down next to him.

"I hope this is a social visit, because I don't have my journal," I said with a smile.

Sam let out a laugh and then said, "Jason couldn't see me, could he?"

"Nope," I replied.

"Does this bother you, Stan?" he asked.

"To be honest, I was hoping he could see you, so I could convince myself that I wasn't hallucinating."

"Cooper can see me," he said as he reached over and gave him a pat on the head.

"Is that supposed to make me feel better?" I asked with a laugh.

Sam gave out a chuckle and then we watched the kids for a few minutes.

"They look good. You have done a good job with them," he said.

"Thanks. They are good kids," I replied.

"Do you remember what I said to you last year when we were sitting in this very place?"

I wasn't sure which conversation he was talking about, so I didn't give an answer.

After a moment, he answered his own question. "Maybe you need them just as much as they need you."

"Ah yes. I got pretty mad at you, didn't I?" I said.

"Do you remember one of the rules of the principle of self-initiative?" he asked.

I thought for a second, and then it came to me.

"Yes—to remember that anything you do to, or for, another, you do to, or for, yourself. Because your every thought or every act which benefits or injures another person comes back to you in kind, greatly multiplied," I stated.

He smiled at me. "Yes, Stanley. Do you think that the time and effort you have put into these kids has brought you any dividends?" he asked.

"Yes, more than I could have ever expected," I said.

Sam continued, "The principles are laws that have been in place since the beginning of time. They work just as much today as they did when they were spoken into existence."

"I am beginning to see that," I said.

"Yes, Stanley, you are," he said.

Just then, Jason hit a hard grounder to the third base player, who picked it up and threw it to first base.

"Out," we both said at the same time.

We smiled at the event.

"Well, Stanley, we need to talk a little business. On Monday, you will need to take a little trip. You are going to go to Ada, Oklahoma to meet a very special man who has been a carrier of The Message for a very long time. His name is Harland Stonecipher. He is the founder of Pre-Paid Legal. He has experienced great success in his business and in his life. His success is much like yours."

I looked over at Sam.

"Like mine?" I asked.

"Yes—much like you, The Message came to him in the midst of adversity."

I nodded my head in understanding.

"I don't want to say too much, so I will let you hear about it from him. Go see him at 10:00 A.M. He will be expecting you."

I sat there for a moment, and then I said, "Thanks, Sam. I better get back to practice."

He smiled at me and said, "I'll see you later."

I kind of expected him to disappear or something, but he just sat there. I got up and walked back to the kids and called them in for some batting practice.

When I looked back up, he was gone. I don't know if I will ever get used to that.

On Monday morning, I got up at 6:30 A.M. I had to be on the road by 7:15, because it was about a two-and-half-hour drive to Ada from Tulsa, and I didn't want to be late for my meeting.

When I arrived, I was amazed at what beautiful structures the Pre-Paid Legal offices were. They stood as a monument on top of a large hill, just on the outskirts of town. I walked into the huge, glass-walled lobby and was greeted by the secretary at the front desk. I told her who I was, and she asked me to take a seat for a moment. I sat in the chair and took in the splendor of it all. About five minutes went by, and a young gentleman stepped out of the elevator and greeted me.

"Hello, Mr. Walters. My name is John. I will take you to meet Mr. Stonecipher."

Just Believe

We walked back to the same elevator he had just come from. He swiped his card and pushed the top button marked Executive Level. As we stepped out of the elevator, I was impressed with the awards and artwork that covered the walls. Most impressive was the six-foot Lady Justice statue in the corner of the room.

We walked and entered the office at the end of the hall. Mr. Stonecipher was sitting at his desk as we entered.

"Mr. Walters," he said as he stood up to great me.

He was a distinguished-looking man dressed in a finely tailored suit. If I had to guess, I would say he was in his late 60s.

"Please come in," he welcomed.

We entered the nicely furnished office. It was at the top of the building on the corner. It had two full walls of glass overlooking the beautiful rolling terrain of Ada, Oklahoma. We walked over to a nice sitting area that consisted of two lounge chairs and a coffee table. His walls were covered with pictures of his family.

"How was your trip down?" he asked.

"Fine, thank you," I replied. John left the room and Harland turned to me.

"I see you brought your journal."

I looked down at it and said, "Yes, I have learned that I need to have this with me at all times."

"You never know when you will need it," he said with a smile.

"Stanley, I am glad you could come today because I have some vital information to share with you about The Message. The principle that I want to share with you is the one of overcoming adversity. This principle has a special place in my heart because this principle was my introduction to The Message. Let me take you back to the moment I discovered it.

"In 1969, I was involved in an automobile accident that wasn't my fault. It was a bad accident that destroyed both vehicles but also caused bodily injury to myself and the other driver. In fact, we both landed in the hospital for quite some time. The other car made an improper turn in front of me, and I was going about 65 miles an hour, and we ended up hitting head-on.

"This was a turning point in my life. As I lay in the hospital, I realized how close I was to death and how fortunate I was. I was just thankful to be alive. Now this is where my story gets interesting.

"I was in the hospital and the costs were being covered by my health insurance. My car was totaled, and it would also be covered by insurance, but I was just simply not prepared for a lawsuit. The fact is that even though the accident was the other driver's fault, she sued me. I didn't even know a lawyer at the time, and I was concerned about the cost to defend myself. I really didn't have the money to get involved in a long, drawn-out legal battle. In fact, I was forced to borrow some money from my relatives so I could hire a lawyer to defend myself.

"As a result of this tragic event, I realized that most Americans are just like I was that morning when I left to go to work. They are not thinking that they will have to defend themselves in a court of law. Not only are they not thinking about it, most are totally unprepared in the event that they may need a lawyer.

"That situation, that adversity in my life, is what gave me the idea for Pre-Paid Legal. Every person that you know has had one event or another that they would see as an adversity. It could be anything such as losing a job or a loved one, or a car accident. The real question is what you will do with that event in your life. I could have been the victim, created a case for myself as to why I couldn't get ahead in life, and blame it all on the accident. Many people do just that. They build a story around an event and stop growing or living because of it. Adversity can be the thing that defines who you are, or it can become a stepping-stone to success. In this adversity, I was able to find the seed of an equivalent benefit.

"I have heard it said that learning from adversity makes it possible for you to redirect all your past failures and mistakes into an asset that will help you achieve outstanding success in the future. There is one thing that I want to point out as I go into explaining the principle of overcoming adversity. Having a positive mental attitude is the only means by which you can convert adversities, defeats, and failures into assets. It seems to me that everyone will experience, or has experienced, adversities, defeats, and even failures as part of this grand experience we call life. It seems that these events are a way of disciplining people to take possession of their own minds. But the Creator, very wisely it seems, provided everyone with the means for converting these experiences into benefits of a priceless value—the means being our ability to maintain and direct a positive mental attitude.

"Despite the benefits that we receive from adversities and unpleasant experiences, no one enjoys when these events take place."

He paused for a moment as if he was trying to formulate his next thought.

"Stanley, I know that the loss of a loved one at any age is usually regarded as an irreparable loss which offers no possible benefit."

I stopped writing at this sentence and looked up at him. I could see the compassion in his eyes. I could see that what he was saying was hard for him to say, but it was a subject that must be broached. He continued.

"But even in the loss of loved ones, we will find that there is a seed of an equivalent benefit. Please understand me when I say this, Stanley. You may have to look hard for it, which is hard for anyone in that position. This is true because you are forced to look through your pain, and that can be a very cloudy state of vision. But trust me when I tell you if you look hard enough, you will find that seed of equivalent benefit.

"Please remember this one thing about adversities. Nothing is ever so bad, or so unpleasant, that it may not yield some benefit if we keep a positive mental attitude toward the experience and make it a habit to look for that seed of an equivalent benefit. This, of course, involves the application of that important success principle, personal initiative. I think you may have learned of that principle already."

Just Believe

I nodded "yes" to him.

"Stanley, you must understand that finding the seed in any adversity is something that must be practiced. It is like anything else in the world that will go away if it is not used. For example, tie your arm to your side and take it out of use. Eventually it will atrophy, wither, and become useless. Neglect to keep in contact with your friends, and you will lose them. Show indifference to your customers, and very soon you will find yourself without a market for your services. It is an inevitable law of nature that you will lose that which you do not use. Of course, this applies to the use of your own mind. Stop feeding it and challenging it, and it will slowly become idle.

"During our time together, I have unveiled the principle of overcoming adversity. The idea of profiting from adversity may have been a surprise or shock to you. If you are ready for this principle, you will embrace it at once and never again, as long as you live, will you brood over unpleasant experiences without knowing full well that your efforts could be better employed by searching for that seed of an equivalent benefit which is available in every experience of adversity.

"Stanley, I would like to give you an assignment before you go. If you dare take advantage of it sincerely, it will bring you a new birth of opportunities that you never dreamed you could experience. Are you ready for this?" he asked.

I stopped writing for a second and had to think about it. Thinking of adversity in my life could bring up some bad memories and bad feelings, but I thought I was ready for it.

"Yes, I am," I agreed.

"Good! I want you to go back into your past experiences, study each adversity and failure you might have experienced, and look for that seed of an equivalent benefit you may not have seen or discovered. You may find yourself richer than you believed yourself to be. You see, riches are much more than money or possessions. True riches cannot be measured by material possessions; they are stored in your heart and mind. They can be recalled at any time, and they teach us every moment if we allow them to. True riches are the moments that we live within and store in our hearts.

"I know this was a tough visit for you," he continued, "but I believe a necessary one. It is through trials that we discover who we really can be. Too many times we see ourselves as less valuable when we experience trials in our lives."

He reached into his pocket and pulled out a $100 bill.

He looked at me and asked, "Stanley, would you like to have this $100 dollar bill?"

"Yes," I said. "Who wouldn't?"

Then he took the bill and crumpled it up into a wrinkly pile in his hand.

"Do you still want it?" he asked.

"Yes, of course," I said.

He then took the bill and threw it on the ground. He took his right foot and began to stomp on it until it was a flattened, wrinkled mess.

"How about now?"

I was a little confused, but I answered, "Yes."

"Why do you want it, Stanley? Can't you see that it has been beaten up and treated badly? It is hardly recognizable."

"Yes, I understand that, but it is still 100 bucks," I said.

He smiled big at me.

"Exactly, it still has the same value, no matter what adversity it may have experienced. Too many times we let the mistakes, setbacks, any type of adversity, or circumstances dictate our value as people. Stanley, you are as valuable as you were the day you experienced your greatest adversity. You are now even more valuable because you recognized and acted on the seed of equivalent benefit."

He stopped to let that sink in for a moment. I had stopped writing when he flashed the $100 bill in front of me, so I had to catch up.

He leaned forward in his seat and gave me one last comment.

"I want to leave you with one last thought. Real growth in life only comes from overcoming adversity. Don't feel as though you are being punished when moments of adversity come to your life. Be very careful not to fall into a victim mentality when adversity comes. Be sure to keep your eye out for the equivalent benefit and you will find it. This practice will turn every situation into a stepping-stone of growth for you."

Overcoming Adversity

He stood up, shook my hand, and I was on my way home.

The two-and-a-half-hour drive home seemed to fly by. I had a lot to think about. I didn't realize how much equivalent benefit had come out of my greatest adversity in life.

Losing a child is the most devastating thing that can happen to anyone. For two years, I let that loss define who I was. I did not live for those two years; I only existed. I would venture to say that I just barely survived. When I was able to believe that there was a future, I was able to get out of my self-imposed prison. It just took a willingness to see things differently.

Now I am the father of two beautiful girls. I am working on a book that has the potential to change peoples' lives forever. My story is being made into a movie that will present the world with The Message of *"Just Believe."* All this has happened because I was able to see the seed of equivalent benefit from adversity. If I had the chance to do it all over and not lose Eddy, I would make that choice. But those choices are not up to us, and we can turn them into a benefit if we are willing to do so.

When I arrived home, the girls had held dinner for me. They were very excited to hear what the next principle was going to be. I took out my journal and read my notes as we ate dinner. I could tell that this particular principle hit home with all of us. Each one of us sitting at that table had experienced a big adversity.

They all thanked me for sharing when I was done, and Rachael spoke up for the first time.

Just Believe

"When my parents died in the fire, I never thought that I would every be happy again. When I met you guys and Cooper, I guess you could say that I found the seed of the greater benefit. I am just happy that we got to live next to you," she said.

I looked over at Lisa. She was wiping her eyes.

I smiled at her, and she said, "Boy, the pollen is really bad this time of year."

We all laughed at her comment. Then we cleared the table and got ready for bed.

That night, I kissed the girls good night, and we said our prayers. Josh gave us an example of praying with enthusiasm. It made me feel as if I were at a Shakespearean play. I have not heard so many thees and thous before in my life. She was very entertaining.

As I walked out of the room, I noticed her poster.

The Principles of The Message
1. Faith
2. Personal Initiative
3. Self-Discipline
4. Go The Extra Mile
5. Enthusiasm
6. Overcoming Adversity

Chapter Seventeen

Positive Mental Attitude

"There is little difference in people, but that little difference makes a big difference. The little difference is attitude. The big difference is whether it is positive or negative."

W. Clement Stone

I had been working on my book for about a week without any more visits from Charles, Sam, or any of the other messengers. It made me wonder if the visits were all done. Charles spoke of ten principles, and I had only received six. I should have learned by then that when I start doubting or questioning the goings on of my new mentors that my questions would be answered shortly.

I was typing away on my computer in the office when I received a phone call.

"Is this Stanley Walters?" the lady on the other end of the phone asked.

"Yes. How can I help you?" I replied.

"Please hold for Mr. Forbes," she requested.

Who did she say? Did she just say *Mr. Forbes*? As I listened to the hold music, questions raced through my head.

"Hello, Stanley," came a voice on the phone.

"Yes, this is Stanley Walters," I said, and as I did, I felt like a fool. He knew who I was.

"Stanley, I was wondering if you and I might have a visit soon?"

"Yes, that would be great," I said.

"Perfect. Would it be all right with you if we met at my offices here in New York?" he asked.

"Yes, when would you like to meet?" I asked.

"Don't concern yourself with travel. I will have my office make all the arrangements. Can you meet next Tuesday at 2 P.M.?" he asked.

"Yes, that will be great."

"Superb. I look forward to it. Stay on the line, and my assistant will be right with you to make the arrangements."

The hold music returned, and then the voice of the friendly lady was back. She took down all of my information and told me that she would email my itinerary to me by the end of the day.

"Thanks," was all I could say.

I was blown away by the possibility of meeting Steve Forbes.

I had a week before I was set to leave for New York, so I planned on using the time to work on the book some more. At least that is what I thought I was going to do until my phone rang once again. There was a man on the other end of the line.

"Hello. Stanley Walters please," he said.

"This is Stanley Walters."

"Hello Stanley. I am calling at the prompting of a mutual friend of ours."

He paused for a second to let it sink in.

"Let me guess. Charles Montgomery III?" I responded.

"You are correct. Have you got some time this afternoon to meet?" he asked.

"I sure do," I replied.

He gave me his information. His name was Kyle Hawkins. He asked me to meet him at his gym, All-time Fitness. I knew his name through Lisa, since she was in the fitness business. He was one of the youngest owners in the franchise, and he owned several locations.

I arrived at 1 P.M. as he had requested, and I was impressed by the look of his gym. It was a large location in a nice, clean environment. I walked in the front door and was greeted by a friendly young girl who looked to be in her late teens. I told her I was here to see Kyle, and she picked up the phone and paged him.

"Kyle to the front please. Kyle to the front."

She hung up the phone and went back to working on some paperwork.

From behind me I heard a voice call out, "Stan."

I turned around and I saw a good-looking, fit young man who happened to be in a wheelchair. I must have had a surprised look on my face.

"Not what you expected, huh?" he said.

I felt bad for broadcasting my surprise on my face.

Just Believe

"No, ah, what do you mean?"

I was backpedaling, but it didn't matter. The fact was I had a surprised look on my face and it showed.

"Don't feel bad," he said. "It happens all the time. People don't expect a gym owner to be in a wheelchair. Come on into my office, and we can visit."

We walked down a short hallway to a nicely-equipped office. He wheeled in behind his desk. He looked at a Post-it note for a second and then looked up at me.

"I guess by now you know why I called you," he said.

"Yes. You will be the seventh messenger that I have met with."

"Good. How has your experience been so far?" he asked.

"Pretty crazy, actually. Next week I am going to meet with Steve Forbes," I said.

"Really? I have not had the honor. I hear he is an amazing thinker."

He paused for a second to catch his thoughts.

"Stanley, do you have any idea which principle I am going to share with you?" he asked.

"To be honest, I would have guessed overcoming adversity, but that happened last week."

He smiled. "That is actually one of my favorites, but there is another principle that I love to share that carried me through one of the toughest times in my life."

I had the feeling that the lesson was going to start, so I opened my journal and took out my pen.

"I was not always in this chair, Stanley. At one time in my life, I was a very active, athletic young man who thought he had the world by the tail. I loved the outdoors and I loved all kinds of sports. I used to water ski, snow ski, wakeboard, snowboard, run, rock climb, and so on. If it was a challenge, I was up for it. My parents used to try to get me to take it easy, and not take so many chances, but I was full steam ahead or nothing.

"When I was 18 years old, I was at the river with my friends. We were swimming and playing on a rope swing. We were all taking turns trying to impress each other by doing different tricks and flips off of the swing. I was particularly good at flips.

"The river was not large. It was actually only about 50 feet across, but it was about 10 feet deep in the middle. It was one of my favorite places.

"The water was cool and pretty clear. Sometimes when you were high up on the rope swing, you could look down and see fish. It was actually kind of freaky when you came down on top of them. One of my friends actually got a fin in his foot. It hurt pretty bad, but it made a great battle scar and story to impress the girls."

He let out a laugh, and I had to laugh, too. This guy was full of energy and enthusiasm. I was really enjoying his story.

"Anyway, like I said, I was out there with my friends, and we were trying to impress each other. I had this idea of climbing way up in the tree, higher than anyone else had gone, to see how high I could get in the air on the swing. My friends were all telling me I was crazy, but that made me want to do it all the more. I was way up in the tree, and I launched out on the swing. I had not intended to let go at the end, I was just going to hang on and swing back. As I went flying down toward the water, I could feel the speed and force pulling me from the rope. By the time the rope reached the end of its arc, I was about 30 feet in the air. The centrifugal force was more than I could withstand, and I lost grip of the rope.

"It was one of those moments that you will always remember. It was like everything went into slow motion. I had swung so far out that I was all the way across the river and headed toward the other shore. It seemed like I floated in the air for 10 minutes before I started to fall to the ground. I was falling headfirst and I remember thinking to myself that I needed to rotate so I landed on my back and not my head. I flailed my arms around to try to turn my body. I was only able to rotate about a quarter of the way before I hit the water. I landed on my right shoulder in about 6 inches of water. I remember my body folding in half as I hit, and I distinctly remember the loud 'CRACK' sound that came from my back. Then everything was still and quiet.

"My friends ran and swam over to me as quick as they could. One of them happened to be a nurse, and she kept me still as I lay in the water. She kept telling me that everything was going to be OK, but I knew I couldn't feel or move anything below my chest. I knew that my life would never be the same."

He paused for a moment and then continued. "That was 10 years and about a dozen operations ago. I have been very fortunate."

He stopped again and then he pointed to a drawing on the wall. It was a regular piece of white copy paper in a nice wooden frame. On the paper was a hand sketch of three letters PMA.

"Do you see that drawing on my wall?" he asked.

I turned to look at it.

"Yes," I answered.

"I drew that when I was in the hospital about two months after the accident. Do you have any idea what they stand for?" he asked again.

I studied them for a moment and tried to formulate an answer.

"Not really, no. What do they stand for?" I asked.

"PMA: Positive—Mental—Attitude," he said boldly. "That is what got me through dealing with the loss of the use of my legs, and it is what continues to allow me to prosper in my life today. Of course, I had to learn the principle of overcoming adversity, which was actually very easy for me. But it was my PMA that carried me through some of the most trying and actually painful times in my life. I would like to share the principle of PMA that was given to me from a very wise man—if that would be OK with you?"

I was actually surprised he asked me.

"Yes, by all means. I am ready to go," I held up my journal as I spoke.

"Great. First of all, you need to understand the power of a PMA. It has the power to clear away all obstacles that stand between you and your major purpose in life. Trust me, Stanley. As far as I am concerned, having a PMA is the most important of all the ten principles of The Message. I want to give you a list of ways that you can obtain and maintain a good Positive— Mental— Attitude. Are you ready?"

I could tell that he coached a lot of people in his life.

"Yes!" I let out.

"OK, here we go:

- "To have a Positive Mental Attitude, you need to adjust yourself to other people's states of mind and difficulties. This allows you to get along peacefully with others. Also try to refrain from making a big deal out of little things when it comes to relating to other people. Great people always avoid small issues when it comes to other people.

- "To have a Positive Mental Attitude, you need to establish a definite fixed system of conditioning your mind at the beginning of each day so that you can condition your mind to be positive in all circumstances. I like to start my day out with meditation and thankfulness. I think of all the things that I am thankful for, and I thank God for each one. Do this every morning. You will find that you miss it if you skip a day.

- "To have a Positive Mental Attitude, you need to avoid unimportant arguments over unimportant subjects. You need to have a clear mind that is not interested in petty issues.

- "To have a Positive Mental Attitude, you need to adopt the habit of having a good hearty laugh every time you become irritated or angry. This may seem like a strange thing to do, but trust me, it will change your attitude quickly. I also like to start the day with at least one minute of laughing. This actually changes the chemistry of your brain and will start you out with a PMA for the day.

- "To have a Positive Mental Attitude, you need to learn to start each day by expressing gratitude for all the adversities, defeats, and failures that you have experienced in the past. Then give thanks for the equivalent seeds of benefit that have come to you through the passing of time. Also give thanks for the blessing you plan to receive during the day. You will find that you see what you are focused on. If you decide to focus on the good that comes out of bad, you will see it. If you focus on just the bad, that is all you will see and all you will have.

- "To have a Positive Mental Attitude, you need to learn to concentrate your attention on the 'Can-Do' portion of all of your problems and desires. Then start to work on them where you stand and put into action what you can with what you have. No matter what may be your problem or your desire, there is always something you can do right now that will help you. Find out what the some-thing is and then do it.

- "To have a Positive Mental Attitude, you need to learn to redirect all unpleasant circumstances into immediate action. Apply your PMA and learn to make this a fixed habit. For example, when you are angry, switch your mind to some sort of action that is in connection with something you enjoy, maybe a hobby or your major purpose in life. Keep your mind busy with that subject for at least five minutes.

- "To have a Positive Mental Attitude, you need to learn to recognize that every circumstance that influences your life, whether it is a pleasant or unpleasant circumstance, is food for your mental attitude. Learn to use it to make it pay you dividends in one form or another. Remember that your strength grows out of your struggle. Do this and you will learn that there is no such thing as an unprofitable experience.

- "To have a Positive Mental Attitude, you need to see your life as continuing education. You can learn from all of your experiences, good or bad. Keep an eye out for little grains of wisdom that are found in each circumstance. If you look for them, you will find them.

- "To have a Positive Mental Attitude, you need to work to be patient, kind, and more generous with others. Treat others as you would like to be treated.

- "To have a Positive Mental Attitude, you need to make it a habit to always express gratitude that you have been given the ultimate gift in having the ability to have complete control over your own mind. Ask for guidance in order that you may use this amazing gift wisely in all of your thoughts and actions.

- "To have a Positive Mental Attitude, you need to go out of your way, at least once a day, to comment enthusiastically on the good qualities of those in your inner circle. This would include your family, friends, and co-workers. Be sure not to mention any negative qualities. When you do this, you will start to see how quickly others will begin to do the same to you. This is one of the main keys to keeping your mind positive.

- "To have a Positive Mental Attitude, you need to accept all criticism as an opportunity for self-examination to determine how much of it is justified. If you are willing to listen without being offended, you will discover things about yourself that can be adjusted and will help you throughout your entire life.

- "To have a Positive Mental Attitude, do not accept anything that you do not want in your life. You have the ability to deny anything you do not want to be a part of your life just the same way you have the ability to accept the thing you do want.

- "To have a Positive Mental Attitude, you need to remember that there are only two types of circumstance that cause you to worry: those that you can do something about, and those you can do nothing about. Learn to identify the difference between the two. Change those you can, and learn from those you can't.

- "To have a Positive Mental Attitude, you need to keep your mind engaged on the things that you want the most or your major purpose in life. This way, there will be no time left for you to waste on thinking on the things that you do not want.
- "To have a Positive Mental Attitude, never put yourself in the position of feeling sorry for yourself. Look around until you find someone who is worse off than you. Figure out a way to help that person, and then do it. Make this procedure a habit, and you will witness one of the great miracles of life, because that which you do to or for another, you do to or for yourself.
- "To have a Positive Mental Attitude, you need to choose someone that you consider to be the type of person that you would like to be. Then go to work and emulate that person in every way possible. If you want to be a success in life, do the things successful people do. I know it sounds simple, but it is very effective.
- "To have a Positive Mental Attitude you need to write out the following sentence and paste it in several places where you will see it each and every day. *Whatever the mind can conceive and believe, the mind can achieve.* Say this to yourself every time you see the notes. This statement is the foundation to success in life.

"I know this seems like a lot of information, but these 19 points have been time tested and proven in millions of people's lives over the years. You must also remember that you are the only person on earth who can provide you with a positive mental attitude. No one can give it to you or take it away from you. You are the master of your own mind."

I thanked him for his time and, after a tour of the facility, I headed to school to pick up the girls. As is tradition, Josh jumped in the front seat and Rachael in the back. I hid my journal from Josh. When she got in the car, she looked around to see if I had it with me. I didn't say anything. Josh was going to be staying overnight at her friend Alex's house that night, so we needed to get home so she could get her stuff.

"So, what did you do today?" she asked.

"You know, the norm," I responded.

"You didn't meet anyone today?" she asked.

I let the question hang for a moment. She started to lift her arms as if to say, *Well, I'm waiting...*

"I didn't say that," I admitted. She started to look around for the journal again and opened the glove compartment to reveal its hiding place.

"I can't believe you would do that to me," she protested. I let out a hearty laugh.

She quickly scanned through the pages to get to today's notes. She read them out loud to us as we drove home, and we discussed how we could put this principle into action to help us to have a positive mental attitude. When we arrived home, the girls gave Lisa all the details over dinner, then Lisa took Josh to Alex's for the night and I put Rachael to bed. That night after we said our prayers, I looked at Josh's poster. Number seven was yet to be added to the list. I took her pen and wrote it on there for her.

The Principles of The Message
1. Faith
2. Personal Initiative
3. Self-Discipline
4. Go The Extra Mile
5. Enthusiasm
6. Overcoming Adversity
7. Positive Mental Attitude

Chapter Eighteen

Accurate Thinking

"As a man thinks, so is he."
Proverbs 23:7 (paraphrase)

The next few days flew by quickly. We had two baseball practices over the weekend, and each time I kept an eye out for Sam.

Monday came, and I caught my flight from Tulsa to Newark. It was nice to take a direct flight. Mr. Forbes flew me first class and then had a limo waiting to take me to my hotel. I had never been to New York, so the whole experience was grand. When I got to the hotel, there was a welcome basket on the table with a hand-written note from Mr. Forbes.

I look forward to our meeting.—Steve

The next morning, I rose early and walked around town a little. I was just off 46th Street and Broadway, so I was between Rockefeller Center and Times Square. It was a clear day, and the temperature was around 65 degrees. I decided to kill some time by walking around Manhattan. I walked through Times Square and through the Broadway show district. Then I made my way over to the observation deck at Rockefeller Center, 30 Rock (a local told me it was called that).

I took the tour that went to the top of the building. It was an amazing view. Seeing Manhattan from 60 stories up can change anyone's perspective. It is a work of art. To the north you could see Central Park, and to the south you could see the Brooklyn Bridge, Times Square, and even the Statue of Liberty.

I took a moment to practice what Kyle said and I expressed my gratitude for all of the things that I was learning and for all of the blessings in my life. It is amazing how this simple act can set your mind and heart in the right perspective. As I thought about the past few weeks and even the past couple of years, I realized that one of the biggest changes in me was my new sense of spirituality. I had never been a religious man, but now I would consider myself a spiritual man. The practice of praying with the girls before they go to bed, and now having a moment every morning of expressing gratitude for the blessings in my life, has given me a sense of closeness with the Creator. I have to think that The Message is a gift from Him to humankind. It is almost a key to unlock the recipe for true success in this time we are given on earth that we call life.

I had to laugh at myself; this was some pretty deep thinking for a Little League baseball coach from Tulsa. I looked down at my watch. It was just before 1 P.M. and I needed to get back to the hotel to be picked up for my 2 P.M. meeting.

Accurate Thinking

I was picked up at the hotel by the limo that Mr. Forbes sent. I have to be honest. I could get used to that type of lifestyle.

We arrived at the building with ten minutes to spare. When I got there, I was escorted to Mr. Forbes' private library and asked to wait for him. I looked around the room. It was probably 15 feet by 15 feet. Every wall except the outside wall, which was glass overlooking the street, was covered with shelves that were filled with books. I would guess there were at least 1,000 books total. In the middle of the room was a circular wooden table that had four chairs. On many of the shelves, there were awards and commendations for achievement. There was even an American flag displayed that had been carried on Air Force One on a day when Mr. Forbes met with President Reagan on the plane. It was all very impressive.

I was reading one of the plaques when Mr. Forbes walked in the room. He greeted me with a big smile and a firm handshake.

"Stanley, it is so good to meet you," he said as he motioned for me to sit at the table.

"Mr. Forbes," I said, "the pleasure is all mine. Thank you for asking me to come, and thank you for arranging all of the travel and accommodations. This is more than I could have ever expected."

"Please, call me Steve," he said. "I am truly honored to meet one of the newest messengers. Charles speaks highly of you. This is the least I could do."

I was a little surprised by the Charles statement.

"Do you speak with Charles often?" I asked.

He thought about it for a moment and then replied, "Only when it is necessary."

I pulled out my journal and pen and got ready to write. He got comfortable in his chair and then began.

"Many people think that, because I was born into this family, everything I have was given to me without any effort on my part. It is true that I have been very fortunate in my life, but there is one thing people should understand. To whom much is given, much is expected. You see, I am not the first carrier of The Message in my family. In fact, I am third generation. My father was a great man, and his father before him. They passed down the principles of The Message from one generation to the next. I have been afforded many opportunities in my life, but without The Message I can guarantee you that I would not have been able to maintain them, let alone grow them and multiply them. My father was a deep thinker and he always emphasized the importance of accurate thinking.

"I have heard it said that accurate thinking is based on two simple fundamentals. They are called inductive reasoning and deductive reasoning. Inductive reasoning is used when the necessary facts you base your thinking on are not available. In this case, you act on hypothesis, or what you may assume the facts to be. Deductive reasoning is used when you have all the facts, or what appear to be the facts, on which to base your thinking.

"The next step to accurate thinking is to separate fact from fiction, or hearsay evidence. You need to determine if you are dealing with hypothesis or real facts. When you are sure you have dependable facts on which to base your line of thinking, you take the second step by separating these facts into two classes: one, the important facts, and two, the unimportant facts. When you do this, you may be surprised at the amount of unimportant facts you deal with on a daily basis.

"If you are like me, you want to cut right to the chase. You want to know: *What is an important fact?* and *How can you distinguish it from an unimportant fact?*"

He paused for a second and slightly smiled at me.

"It is relatively simple actually. An important fact is any fact that will aid you to any extent whatsoever in obtaining the object of your major purpose in life. All other facts, as far as you are concerned, are unimportant, and you should waste no time to even consider them. As a matter of fact, I would wager that you would make a profound discovery regarding accurate thinking if you follow the habit of daily taking inventory of all the things that get your attention during the day. Write them down on a piece of paper in two separate columns. Label one *important facts* and the other *unimportant facts*. It is a good exercise that will most likely show you that most of your thinking energy is spent on thoughts that have nothing to do with aiding you in accomplishing your major purpose in life.

"One of my favorite books tells us to 'take every thought captive.' You will find that once you learn this habit, you will see exponential growth in obtainment of short-term and long-term goals.

Just Believe

"There is another thing that you must take into consideration when it comes to accurate thinking—the subject of opinions. Many times, people will give you information that is wrapped up in the package of fact, but when you delve a little deeper into it, you realize that many times it is nothing more than that person's or that organization's opinion. This being the case, it is a good idea to recognize what opinion actually is. In most cases, opinions are without value, because they are based on personal bias, prejudice, intolerance, guesswork, hearsay evidence, and out-and-out ignorance.

"Once, I was told of a question that was asked of Woodrow Wilson when he was president during World War I. He was asked what effect he thought World War I would have on civilization. His answer was most profound, and you can use it as an example about how you should think when you are asked questions. He said. 'I cannot answer that question because I have no facts on which to base an opinion.'

"Try to remember this answer whenever you are given the opportunity to express an opinion about anything. It is a good example to follow and will teach you to not give an opinion unless you have substantial facts or experience to support your opinion. Any other answer would be based solely on your own bias, prejudices, and emotions, which in most cases are never facts.

"You will notice, now that you are aware of accurate thinking, that the more successful a person is, the less they are inclined to express an opinion about anything unless it can be followed up with personal experience and facts. You will also notice that those who have not achieved any level of true success are full of opinions on about every subject you can imagine."

He paused for a moment as I scribbled as fast as I could in my journal. When I finished, he continued.

"I want to give you a simple rule that will protect you from being misled by any unsound opinions. When you hear someone make a statement that you question the accuracy or experience of, ask a simple forward question: *How do you know this?* Then stand firm on that question and either force the person to identify the source from which he got the information that he is trying to pass on as fact, or reject the statement entirely as if it had not been made. This may sound strong, but I would suggest you do this with whomever you meet.

"Remember that you have been given the greatest gift in that you have the ability to control your own thoughts; therefore, it is important for you to treat this divine gift with the utmost respect that it is entitled and not allow anyone to do your thinking for you or to influence your thinking in any manner whatsoever except by the rules of accurate thinking that I have just described to you."

He stopped talking and looked at me as I finished writing. I looked up at him, waiting for the next words to come out of his mouth.

"Stanley, what do you think of what I just told you?"

I didn't anticipate the question, so it took me a moment to answer him.

"This principle, much like the others, is profound and actually much different than how I live now. So to answer your question, I am going to ask you a question about what you have just told me."

He looked at me with expectation. I don't think he expected me to ask him a question.

"Mr. Forbes, I mean Steve, how do you know this?"

When I said that, his face changed from quizzical to humorous. I could tell he liked my boldness and the fact that I was doing exactly what he had told me to do.

"Good question, Stanley. I am happy to answer it with personal experience and facts. The principle of accurate thinking was passed down to me from my father. I am a witness of seeing this principle in action throughout my childhood and into my adult life. I am a subscriber to it today and use it on a daily basis. The personal and financial gain that I have achieved is a direct result of The Message, and the principle of accurate thinking in particular."

He paused for a minute and smiled at me. Then he said "Well done, Stanley; you are a model student."

He got up from his chair and walked over to one of the bookshelves. He searched through some of the books until he put his finger on one in particular. He pulled the book from the shelf and looked at it for a moment. It was bound in leather and looked as though it had seen many years of use. He brought the book over to me and sat down.

"Do you know what this book is, Stanley?" he asked.

I looked down at it. There was no title on the front cover, and it did not look as though it was mass-produced.

"No, I can't say that I do," I replied.

Accurate Thinking

"Stanley, this is my journal. In it are the ten principles of The Message."

It was funny because I looked down at it now with almost a sense of reverence. He opened it and started looking through the pages.

"I started to journal when I was in my early twenties. It all started with the ten principles, and I have continued to journal ever since."

He continued to look through the pages until he found what he was looking for.

"Ah, here it is."

I looked down at the pages and saw a list of seven items.

"Stanley, I want to share with you the seven rules that will guide you to be an accurate thinker."

He looked back down at the page and began to read.

- "An accurate thinker never accepts the opinions of other people as being fact until he has learned the source of those opinions and satisfied himself of their accuracy.
- "An accurate thinker remembers that free advice, no matter from whom it is received, should undergo the closest of examination before it is acted upon as safe. Generally speaking, advice is worth exactly what it costs.
- "An accurate thinker alerts himself immediately whenever he hears someone speaking of others in a destructive or slanderous spirit. The fact that they are speaking in this manner should put

him on notice that what he is hearing is biased, to say the least. In most cases, it is a complete misstatement.

- "An accurate thinker knows when he is asking others for information, he should not tell them what he wishes the information to be. Most people have the bad habit of trying to please under such circumstances. Well-measured, tactful questions can be a great benefit in thinking accurately.

- "An accurate thinker remembers, anything that exists anywhere throughout the universe is capable of proof, and where no such proof is available, it is safe to assume nothing exists.

- "An accurate thinker knows that both truth and falsehood, no matter by what means they may be expressed, carry with them a silent, invisible means of identifying themselves as such; therefore, knowing this he will develop the intuitive faculty to enable him to sense what is false and what is true.

- "An accurate thinker follows the habit of asking, 'How do you know this?' whenever he hears a statement that is not easily identified as truth. Following this habit faithfully will see many persons squirm and turn red in the face when asked for a direct reply to the question."

When he was done with the seventh point, he slowly closed the book as if he were tucking a child away in bed for the evening. He rubbed his hand across the cover and then looked back up at me. This time, his face showed a sense of seriousness that he had not expressed during our meeting.

"Stanley, there is one final word of warning that I feel I should leave with you before you go. Be sure to study yourself carefully, and you may discover that your own emotions are your greatest handicap in the principle of accurate thinking. It is easy to believe what you wish to believe, and unfortunately that is what most people do. Be on the lookout when you form opinions to make sure it is based on fact and not emotion, or you will taint your thought process and eventually base your beliefs on what you want something to be and not on what it actually is."

After that statement, I went to writing, and he got up to put his journal back in its place.

"I take this book out at least four times a year and read all of the principles. I do it at the change of the seasons, and I find that I discover something new every time I read it. Life has its seasons, and truth will always complement each season we experience. I would suggest you do the same with your journal, Stanley. Truth is a power source that, when we stay tapped into it, grows us, much like the sun does for plants. When we stop feeding our minds, we stop growing and eventually wither up and die."

"Thank you, Steve." I said. "I will do that."

He walked back over to me, and I stood up. We shook hands, said our good-byes, and before I knew it I was on a plane headed back to Tulsa.

Just Believe

As the plane was taking off, I looked at the Manhattan skyline and thought of how all of those buildings each represented the fulfillment of someone's dream. It made me think of what Steve said to me as we were walking out.

"Stanley, be sure to qualify anyone that you take advice from. Fact will always carry with it the evidence of experience. For example, if you wanted to start a magazine and distribute it nationally, you would not go to someone who has not done it before. If you did, they would say it can't be done, it's too much work, or you are unqualified and will fail. Ask me that same question, and I will give you a list of things that you need to do to accomplish your goal. I can do this because I have experience in that arena."

What he said was true. Getting facts from someone who has experience in whatever it is that I want to do is vital to success. Looking at the skyline, I realized that none of those dreams could have been built on opinion. They could only be built based on facts. All of our dreams and major purposes in life are just like those buildings. If they are built on opinion, they will not stand, but if they are built on fact, they will grow and have a firm foundation.

Lisa and the girls picked me up at the airport. When I got in the car, I felt like I was in front of a firing squad with all of the questions. *What was New York like? What did you do? What was Steve Forbes like? Was he nice?* The questions continued all the way home.

Accurate Thinking

When we got home, it was late, so for the girls' bed-time ritual, I read the notes from my journal about accurate thinking.

I am amazed at how much the girls grasp the truths of the different principles. They seem to get a grasp a lot faster than I did.

Josh asked if she could pray that night, so we all closed our eyes and she started.

"God, thank You for allowing us to control our minds. I know this is a great gift and that You gave it to us because You love us. Help me to have accurate thinking in school and when I grow up so I can have a definite major purpose like daddy does. Amen."

I couldn't have said it better myself.

Lisa and I kissed the girls goodnight and went out on the porch to sit and talk before we went to bed. I had installed a porch swing, and it had become one of our favorite spots.

She leaned into me as we sat and then she said, "Stanley, this principle has got me thinking."

"Yeah? How so?" I asked.

"The part where he told you to control your emotions. It made me think about what it was like before we met Charles. You were depressed and couldn't see past your pain. The facts were that you needed to let go of the pain and move on with your life, but your opinion was that what happened was unforgivable and that you had to be punished."

I stared at her for a moment and then said, "I guess you're right. My emotions twisted my thinking, and like

Charles said in the kitchen, I embraced the lie and my life became that lie. It wasn't until I changed my thinking that I was set free from that self-imposed prison."

Lisa nodded her head in agreement. "You did not have accurate thinking then. I think it is important when we are feeling emotional to ask ourselves that question. 'How do you know?' I bet the answer will be, 'Because I feel it is true' and when we look deeper we will realize we are basing our lives on something that is entirely wrong."

We sat in silence for a moment.

Then I looked at her and said, "How do you know that?"

We both laughed, and she snuggled in as we continued to rock on the swing.

Later, as I was getting ready for bed, I peeked in the girls' room. They were like two little angels sleeping peacefully in their beds. There on the wall was Josh's updated poster.

The Principles of The Message
1. Faith
2. Personal Initiative
3. Self-Discipline
4. Go the Extra Mile
5. Enthusiasm
6. Overcoming Adversity
7. Positive Mental Attitude
8. Accurate Thinking

Chapter Nineteen

Napoleon

*"Leadership is the capacity to translate
vision into reality."*

Sam Walton

I awoke at 5 o'clock the next morning. I didn't sleep well through the night. My mind was buzzing at 100 miles an hour. I was thinking of all the principles and all that Steve had told me. I was most impressed with the fact that he had kept his journal and that he still read it on a regular basis. This is a habit that I will continue.

The thought that was going over and over in my head was that I needed to find my definite major purpose. Charles had said this to me when I started the journey, and it has been said to me several times since.

I got up and made some coffee and then went into my office to work for a while. I opened my journal to the inside cover. I wrote down a question: *What is my Definite Major Purpose?* I need to figure this out or all of these principles are for nothing. What is that one thing that defines who I am? I vowed to myself that I would know this before this adventure was over.

Lisa woke up at her usual time and got the girls ready for school. I joined them for breakfast, and we discussed some of the things that we had been learning from the principles. I was listening to Josh and Rachael discuss opinion and fact, and I was amused at how two sisters can take something to the extreme. Rachael was telling us about a field trip her class took to the Tulsa Zoo, and she made the statement that Lions eat 25% of their body weight in meat and can go for up to a week between meals.

Josh had to chime in with, "How do you know that?"

This clearly irritated Rachael, and she responded, "Because they told us at the zoo, thank you very much."

Josh shot back, "Just making sure you're giving me fact and not just opinion."

Lisa and I looked at each other and smiled.

"I think you created a monster," Lisa said to me.

"How do you know that?" I asked, and we all laughed.

After breakfast, Lisa and the girls were off to work and school. I walked back into my office and Cooper was standing there waiting for me with his leash in his mouth. It was time for his walk.

"Sorry, boy, I almost forgot."

I took his leash and attached it to his collar, and we were off to the park. I stepped out the front door and then stopped.

Napoleon

"Wait here, Coop," I said as I ran back into my office and grabbed my journal. I was not going to be caught unprepared again.

It was a beautiful spring day, and the air was crisp and fresh. We took our usual path to the park and worked our way to the wooded area. As I came over the hill, I was happy to see Sam sitting on the bench reading the newspaper.

As I walked up, he noticed me and smiled. He started to fold the newspaper and said, "I am always amazed at the time and energy spent on such trivial items in the reporting of the news. So much resource spent on thought that produces no fruit."

"I guess you're right," I agreed as I sat down next to him.

I made sure to put my journal on my lap out in the open so he could take notice. We sat there silent for a moment watching Cooper chase the squirrels. It almost seemed like it was a game for all of them. He would chase one up a tree and another would come down on the ground and taunt him until he would chase that one up a tree, and the cycle would start all over again.

"He sure loves those squirrels," Sam remarked.

"Yes. I think he just loves life," I said.

"Yes, I would say that is a true statement," Sam agreed.

Then he leaned back in the bench to make himself comfortable. I opened my journal in anticipation of him speaking.

"Before you start writing, I want to talk to you about something that you need to know."

"OK," I said as I closed my journal and laid it on my lap.

He sat there for a moment deep in thought and then looked over at me and said, "Stanley, I am not the man that you think I am."

"I don't understand," I replied.

"I am not a maintenance man that works at the ball field."

I wasn't surprised at all by this statement.

"My name isn't Sam, either. That is a name that I use when on assignment because it fits in better with this current era. My name is actually Napoleon."

He paused. I didn't say anything. I wanted to hear more!

"Stanley, I am much like you. When I was a young child, I endured a tragic event in the loss of my mother. This was very hard on me, and there were times when I didn't think I could overcome the pain of that loss. It wasn't until I was much older that I learned the principles of The Message and was able to see the seed of equivalent benefit from that loss. Then I was able to put that pain to rest. It was at that point I discovered my definite major purpose in life. It is to use all of my physical, spiritual, and mental energies to the proliferation of The Message."

I did not have any words for what I was hearing. I sat and listened intently. This was amazing. If this man was who I thought he was, then I was sitting next to the greatest advocate of The Message in modern history.

"Stanley, now you have but to learn two more principles of The Message. If it pleases you, I would like to share them with you myself."

"Yes, by all means. I would be honored," I agreed eagerly.

He smiled and then stood up.

"Walk with me, Stanley."

I got up and called Cooper over to us. He came running and I attached the leash to his collar. We started walking through the park.

"Do you know why I like this place?" he asked as he looked around. "I like it because it creates an atmosphere. Be sure to always find places in your life that are the right atmosphere for whatever it is you are doing. If you are going to write, go where you feel peaceful and are able to concentrate on what you are doing. In your daily work, be sure to create the right atmosphere with those you spend time with every day. Each one of us has the ability to create the right atmosphere for every stage of our lives. It is a conscious choice. This park has a certain peacefulness about it that allows me to clear my head," he said.

"I know exactly what you mean," I replied.

We continued walking through the wooded area of the park. "Stanley, the next two principles are vital to The Message. If used correctly in conjunction with the other principles, they will all but guarantee your success in any endeavor you put your mind to.

Just Believe

"I want to talk to you about the principle of creative vision. This is the success principle that is responsible for the building of all of our plans, aims, and purposes. It has been said that the imagination is the workshop wherein we fashion the purposes of our brain and the ideals of our soul. I don't know of a better definition.

"You must first understand that there are two forms of imagination.

"First, there is synthetic imagination which consists of organizing and putting together ideas, concepts, and facts arranged in a new combination. Very seldom does anyone create a completely original idea. Nearly everything known to civilization is nothing more than a combination of something that already exists.

"Secondly, there is creative imagination, which operates through the sixth sense and has its base in the subconscious section of the brain. It serves as the exclusive medium through which new ideas or facts are revealed.

"Let me give you an example of synthetic imagination. Henry Ford's first automobile was created by the simple procedure of combining two existing items in a new form. He first took the well-known method of transportation, the horse and buggy, and combined it with the steam-propelled threshing machine. Both ideas were old, but they became a new idea when combined and eventually led to launching a multi-billion-dollar industry that would forever change the world we live in.

"Now I will give you an example of creative imagination. Thomas Edison's invention of the phonograph was the result of creative imagination. No part of his invention had ever been known or used previously.

"You must also understand that there are times when both synthetic and creative imagination work together to create something new. For example, Wilbur and Orville Wright's perfection of the airplane is partly the result of creative and synthetic imagination. Others had previously discovered some of the ideas they used, but the Wright brothers were the first to coordinate those ideas so they worked successfully."

I was following Sam, I mean Napoleon, and writing as fast as I could. I think he noticed the difficulty I was having, so he stopped at the next bench in the park and motioned for me to sit. I sat on the bench while he continued to stand. He took Cooper's leash from me and unhooked the dog to let him run. He continued to stand and started to walk around the bench as he began to talk.

"Please keep in mind when I tell you these principles that the mind—like any other muscle in your body— must be exercised. It will grow dull and useless through disuse and more alert and keen with more use. You are the only one who can supply this action.

"Let me be very clear on this subject. Once you have a vision for something, you are the only one who can take action to bring it to fruition. Use your personal initiative and your self-discipline to bring the thoughts of your imagination to reality. There are some teachings out there that would tell you that all you have to do is think of something many times over, and it will come to you. It is true that the brain lets out vibrations that are either creative or destructive, but those thoughts alone will not create anything tangible. The first and most important step to bringing any creative thought or vision to life is to write it down. I like to quote my favorite book on this subject, 'If you write the vision, it shall surely come.'

"Picture a man who would like to have a tree that yields him a given amount of fruit each season. He cannot sit in his chair and look at the spot thinking to himself, *I want fruit, I want fruit.* No. He must go out and procure the very device that will yield him a harvest of fruit each season. He must find the proper seed and then find the ideal place to plant that seed. Once he does, there will be a period of time where that tree will spread its roots. After a given amount of time, the tree will produce for him the yield of fruit he desired. If the tree is nurtured, it will continue to give to him a greater yield of fruit each season from there on out. This is a principle that has been in existence since the beginning of time, and it has been proven in my life numerous times: Thought without action is pointless.

"Creative vision allows a man to not only see where he currently is in his quest, but it also allows him to see where he wants to be. It allows you to walk into the future with a vision for what you want that future to hold. When you walk in this thought process, you are able to see beyond obstacles that would stop the man with no vision, and you can see where you are going so the obstacles will become inconsequential to you."

He stopped walking for a moment and then sat next to me on the bench. Cooper had now spent all of his energy chasing squirrels and was lying down on the ground next to us.

"Creative vision leads me to the next principle I want to share with you."

I was excited. I had not gotten two principles in one day before.

"But first," he said. "I would like to have some gelato."

"Gelato?" I asked.

"Yes, stracciatella to be exact."

I thought for a second. *Where was the closest gelato store?* He waited patiently as I searched my mind. Then it came to me. There was a little coffee shop I used to frequent called Nordaggio's. If I remembered correctly, they had great homemade gelato.

"I don't know if they have strachia…" I stumbled.

"Stracciatella. Pronounced 'Stratch-ia-tella.' Trust me, Stanley. Once you taste the creamy vanilla with just the right amount of fudge mixed throughout, you will never eat another frozen treat. I discovered it just after World War I when I was in Italy," he said.

"All right then. Let's go," I agreed.

We gathered our stuff and began the walk down the street.

Chapter Twenty

Creative Vision &
Cosmic Habit Force

"Excellence is an art won by training and habituation.
We do not act rightly because we have virtue or excellence, but we rather have those because we have acted rightly.
We are what we repeatedly do.
Excellence then, is not an act but a habit."

Aristotle

We walked in the door of the coffee shop. It was located in the center of a strip mall. The front half of the store was filled with a couple of couches and several overstuffed chairs. The back of the room had a bar with a display case filled with cookies and muffins. On the right side of the bar, there was another display case filled with about a dozen different flavors of gelato. I quickly scanned them and noticed the desired flavor. We ordered two large bowls. The barista was impressed with Napoleon's ability to say the name correctly.

"Not many people can say it the right way," she said.

I could tell Napoleon was very pleased with himself.

We walked out front and found a nice table in the shade. Cooper sat on the ground under the table as we got comfortable and started to eat our treat.

"Ah," he said. "That is good. Just like I remembered it."

I took a bite, and I had to agree with him. It was fantastically creamy gelato with a strong, pure vanilla flavor and frozen chunks of fudge.

"I will be having this again. I can guarantee you that." I said to him.

He smiled big and savored another bite.

We finished off our treat and leaned back in our chairs. I patted my tummy, and Napoleon let out a chuckle. He looked over at the journal sitting on the table, and I took that as my cue that we were going to start up again. I reached over and opened it to the next available page and took out my pen. He cleared his throat and then started back up.

"The next principle that I would like to share with you is the principle of cosmic habit force. Creative thinking is the precursor to this principle because the mind can conceive many things, but without the ability to put them into action, they will wither and die on the vine.

Cosmic habit force is a law of nature that applies to all of our habits, both good and bad. This principle is the law that gives definiteness of action to everything that moves throughout the universe. Please understand that the law of cosmic habit force, like any other law in nature, has both a positive and a negative aspect to it.

The negative side of this law is called hypnotic rhythm. When we neglect to fix our thoughts on the things that we want in our life, the law automatically acts through the negative hypnotic rhythm feature and fixes our mind on the things that we do not desire. This attracts to us the physical counterpart of our desires.

When you are able to fully grasp the principle of cosmic habit force, it will be evident to you that you cannot go through life without using the power of this law to carry out the circumstances and the desires you voluntarily choose, or by your neglect allow the same law to force you to pay the penalty as I have explained it to you.

"I know this is a lot of information that may be hard for you to grasp here in our meeting. Be sure to study what I am telling you, and it will become clear to you over time.

"In short, we are all creatures of habit. If we do not focus on the things we want in life, and commit the obtainment of them to habit, the opposite will happen. By not having good habits in our life, we automatically have bad habits. Cosmic habit force is in action every day of our lives.

"Your everyday thoughts form your habits. Until you make a concerted effort to change them, your mind will operate on what you have fed it to date. You need to remember to apply the principle of accurate thinking to yourself on a regular basis. When you recognize a habit and locate the associated thought that has caused that habit to be in existence, ask yourself: 'How do you know this?' Identify the source of your thought or belief and determine if it is based on fact or fiction.

"You hold within you the most powerful gift given to any living creature. It is the power of choice. Your neglect to exercise it properly will bring certain, if not always swift, retribution upon you. Emerson gives a good description of this law in his paper, *The Law of Compensation*. He stated that nothing ever just happens by luck, but every effect has its definite cause.

"I would like to give you some illustrations that will show you how the law of cosmic habit force operates.

"Cosmic habit force fixes the habits of the electrons and protons in matter so that their relationship and chemical behavior always follow the same pattern. This proves to us that everything throughout the universe comes under the influence of cosmic habit force. Everything moves and exists by a pattern, which is unchangeable and enduring, except when man, by the power of his creative vision, can break the habits established by cosmic habit force that affect him, and set up in their place habits of his own choice.

"Cosmic habit force fixes the pattern of every form of vegetation that grows from the soil of the earth so that each thing reproduces after its own kind. A grain of wheat always reproduces other grains of wheat, but never makes the mistake of producing oats or some other form of growth. An oak tree always springs from an acorn but never from any other cause. The pattern was permanently fixed in the acorn by the law of cosmic habit force.

"When the human mind is focused on its definite major purpose, the law of cosmic habit force goes into action immediately and attracts to the individual the material equivalent of that purpose. This is a law of the universe and never varies; however, hypnotic rhythm—the negative application of cosmic habit force—will most definitely attract to the person all the undesirable things and circumstances that the mind is allowed to dwell upon such as poverty, ill health, failure, and fear.

"Remember, the greatest force to stop any positive motion in one's life is fear. You must also remember that fear is nothing more than a bad habit, and it can be permanently removed from a person's life with the law of cosmic habit force.

"Cosmic habit force, expressing itself through the emotion of sex, is the means by which every living thing perpetuates its species. Understand this truth, and you will better understand the apparently irresistible forces of the profound emotion of sex, the means by which the Creator put in place for all living things to survive.

"I don't know if you have heard the term 'on the beam.' It is when you have established a successful thought pattern in your mind that the law of cosmic habit force has picked up and carried out to its logical conclusion. You know you are 'on the beam' when you take possession of your mind, direct it to definite ends in a spirit of belief in your obtainment of those ends, and keep your mind busy in carrying out your definite purpose, instead of allowing it to drift to subjects you wish to avoid. You are 'on the beam' when you can truthfully say, 'I know precisely what I want from life, and I have faith I shall get it.' You are not on the beam when you have no definite major purpose, and you are drifting aimlessly through life.

"Doctors dread the word fixation. Fixation means that a sick person believes that his sickness is something that cannot be cured. On the opposite side, a fixation can become a priceless asset when you discover that the key to success is the ability to develop a fixation in your mind that is focused on the things you desire most. Cosmic habit force is the power that makes fixations permanent.

"You should have a definite fixation based on your major purpose. You must remember that you are the only one that can create this fixation. You can do it by taking possession of your own mind and keeping it directed toward the obtainment of your major purpose in life. If you do this, you will find that in a short time you will be 'on the beam' and headed directly toward everything you desire and deserve to receive.

"Always remember that your mental attitude is something that only you control, and you must use self-discipline until you create a thought pattern or thought habits that keep your mental attitude positive at all times. Your mental attitude is important because it acts as a magnet that will attract to you everything and every circumstance that defines who you are and what station you hold in life. If you wish to stay 'on the beam' successfully, be sure that you give cosmic habit force a thought pattern based on the things that you desire most in life, and it will do the rest.

"These keys, though they may be as old as time itself, are still as true today as when they were created."

He stopped talking, and I finished up my notes. He looked at me, and it almost seemed as if there was a bit of sadness in his face.

"What is it?" I asked.

"Oh, please forgive a sentimental old man," he said

"For what?" I asked.

"Stanley, this will be my last meeting with you. You now have the ten principles to The Message. You are armed with the secrets to true success and happiness and how to bring them to you. There is nothing that you will not be able to do if you follow these principles and daily apply them to your life."

He paused for a moment and looked down at Cooper sleeping on the ground at his feet.

"I would be a liar if I did not say that I have grown attached to you and Cooper. You are one of the rare ones who grasped The Message early. I believe that you will be one of the greatest proliferators of The Message, and your name will be synonymous with success. I want to thank you for allowing me this time with you. It has been my distinct honor."

He stood up and reached his hand out to me.

"Will I ever get to see you again?" I asked.

He smiled. "That remains to be seen. I am sure if the need arises, I will see you again, but I have a feeling that you are going to do just fine on your own."

Just Believe

Without thought, I stood up, reached over to him, and hugged him. I could tell that he wasn't expecting the gesture, but he returned the embrace with zeal. We stepped apart and shook hands. I looked deep in his eyes and there was a bit of moisture around the rims.

"I want to leave you with one final thought," he said. "Always remember that whatever the mind can conceive and believe it can achieve."

He gave me a big smile and said, "Oh yes, and thank you for the gelato. Best I have had in many years."

With that, he turned and walked away. I watched him as he left, not knowing what to do. I looked down at Cooper who was now awake. He looked back up at me. Then I looked back up to Napoleon, and he was gone once again. I won't ever get used to the disappearing thing.

Chapter Twenty One

The Master Mind

"It is literally true that you can succeed best and quickest by helping others to succeed."

Napoleon Hill

I picked up the girls from school that afternoon. Again Josh jumped in the front seat and Rachael in the back. This time Rachael spoke up first.

"Well Dad, did you meet anyone today?"

"Yes, actually, I got to spend most of the day with Sam."

I told them that Sam is really Napoleon, and I told them the two new principles. Josh read the journal as we drove home. I decided that we should celebrate since I had now received all ten of the principles. I stopped at the nearest health food store and picked up some beautiful T-bone steaks. I am very fortunate that all my girls enjoy a good cut of meat.

Our plan was to surprise Lisa by having dinner on the table when she got home. I pulled the grill out of the garage and got the steaks cooking while the girls tossed some salad and baked some potatoes. Lisa walked in the front door just as I was walking in the back door with the steaks.

"What's the occasion?" she asked.

"I want to celebrate with a nice meal and tell you about the last two principles," I replied.

"I knew it had to be big if you were cooking steaks," she said.

"Why is that?" I asked.

"You usually cook pasta when you did something wrong. Steaks are for celebrating," she said with a sly smile on her face.

"You hush up and get changed," I teased back.

We were sitting around the table enjoying our meal when we heard a noise from the kitchen. We looked up as Charles came walking in the dining room with a plate that had a nice piece of meat on it.

"I hope you don't mind if I join you," he said.

"No, please," we all said.

The girls stared at him as he came in. I hadn't realized this before, but they had never met Charles. They had heard talk of him, but they had never actually seen him before. I was excited and quickly cleared a spot for him at the end of the table. He made himself at home and cut a piece off of the steak and began to eat.

The girls watched him with amazement until he spoke.

"Oh, I do love a good steak. Hormone free at that." We all looked at each other and smiled. We were all glad to have him dine with us.

He continued to eat, and then he dished up some salad and potatoes.

"Mmmmm, that is so good" he said.

I laughed and said, "You messengers really like your food don't you."

"You will find, Stanley, that when you are walking in your definite major purpose you appreciate everything more, especially the small things like steak and warm toast with coffee. We all chuckled and went back to eating. He noticed Josh's poster leaning against the wall. She had updated it when we got home. He took a moment and read it.

The Principles of The Message
1. Faith
2. Personal Initiative
3. Self-Discipline
4. Go The Extra Mile
5. Enthusiasm
6. Overcoming Adversity
7. Positive Mental Attitude
8. Accurate Thinking
9. Creative Vision
10. Cosmic Habit Force

"Very impressive," he said. "Write it down; it shall surely come," he quoted and then went back to eating.

We were finishing up our meal and Charles had found out all about the girls' school, baseball, and books. He showed genuine interest in all they had to tell him. During a break in the conversation, he turned his attention to Lisa and me.

Just Believe

"Well, Stanley and Lisa, now that you have the ten principles of The Message, the important thing that I want to know is: Has your definite major purpose revealed itself to you?"

Lisa looked over at me and then to Charles and said, "I know what mine is."

Charles was intrigued.

"It is to be the best mother that I can be. To instill the ten principles of The Message in their lives and raise them to be carriers of The Message in their own right."

Charles was very pleased with her answer.

"There is nothing more noble than to love your children and to raise them to be more successful than you are in every aspect of life. Just think what they will be able to achieve with the knowledge you will write on their hearts. There is nothing they won't be able to do because they will believe that all things are possible. Good for you, Lisa," he said and then looked over at me.

In fact, everyone looked at me. I guess it was my turn to share.

"Well, for the past few weeks since you told me about finding my definite major purpose, I have been searching to figure out what it is. I kept looking more toward a job or occupation to figure out what kind of work I would want to do. Today, when I was sitting with Sam—I mean Napoleon—it presented itself to me. I am not sure if he noticed it or not, but there was a moment when he was talking, and I could picture myself sitting in his seat saying the words he was saying to someone else. I realized that it has nothing to do with work. I realized it was a lifestyle. It has to be who I am, not what I do.

"My definite major purpose in life is to spread The Message. I want to create and effect a positive change in the lives of every person I come in contact with."

Charles listened intently and smiled as I spoke.

"The thing that solidified it for me was when I came home after the meeting today and started working on my book. I can fulfill my definite major purpose by telling my story through the medium of the written word and through movies."

"Really?" Charles asked.

"Yes," I responded. Jim Stovall and his partner Tracy Trost want to tell our story of loss, redemption, and discovery in a movie. They are going to call it *The Lamp*.

He smiled big and spoke again.

"Stanley, Lisa, it brings me great joy to hear all of this. Again you two have excelled above and beyond my greatest expectations. I can't express how proud I am of all of you."

He looked around the room and included all of us in his statement.

"There is one more thing I want to share with you before you go. Let's call it a bonus principle. As a matter of fact, you are actually already doing it with your relationship with Jim and Tracy."

"Wait, I need to get my journal," I said and jumped up to get it. "Let's sit in the living room so we can be more comfortable."

Just Believe

I came out of my office to see Charles sitting in the overstuffed chair he sat in the first time Lisa had met him. The girls were on the floor, and Lisa was on the couch across the coffee table in front of him. I joined Lisa and opened my journal to the next available page.

Charles took a moment to look at all of us and take in the scene. It was almost as if he was taking a mental picture to recall at a later date.

"For our last lesson together, I want to talk to you about the principle of the master mind."

I wrote down the words "master mind" in my journal.

"A master mind is when two or more people work in perfect harmony for the obtainment of a definite purpose. Let me give you a couple of facts about the master mind that will give you an idea of how important it is and how important it is that you embrace this principle and make it a part of your life, because it will help bring you success in whatever you put your hand to.

"This principle is what allows you to borrow and use the education, experience, influence, and capital of other people in carrying out your own plans in life. This principle is how you can accomplish more in one year than you could accomplish in a lifetime if you had to depend entirely on your own efforts for success. I have heard many men of spiritual training say that the first known application of the master mind was between The Nazarene and His 12 disciples.

"When you form a true master mind alliance with other people, and work with them in a spirit of harmony, you control freely the spiritual forces that are within you in carrying out your plans and desires. The principle of the master mind has the power to give you absolute protection against failure, provided always that your purpose is in using this principle to be beneficial to all you influence. I have had the opportunity to witness the efforts of many men. I can tell you without a doubt that those who experience great amounts of success owe it mainly to their knowledge and application of the principle of the master mind.

"When it comes to those who work for another person or company earning a salary or wages, you have the perfect opportunity to put yourself in a higher income and a more responsible position by forming a master mind alliance with those you work with and with the management. Following the principle of the master mind will allow you to write your own price tag, fix your own wages, establish your own working hours, and give yourself financial independence.

"First, you need to decide definitely where you wish to be and what you wish to be doing during the next three years.

"Second, decide how much money you will be making and what you are going to do to earn it.

"Third, form a master mind alliance with at least one other person in your immediate family, and at least one other among those to whom you are presenting your services.

"By taking these three steps, you will be on your way to bringing about an unlimited amount of financial and personal success. There is no such thing as something for nothing. Everything, including your personal success, has a price that must be paid. The only price you are requested to pay is the effort necessary to do these three simple steps that I have given you.

"Before you take these three steps, there is one thing that you must consider. Always be sure to control your mental attitude. Make yourself friendly and agreeable with everyone you are closely associated with—that is, if you would like friendly cooperation in return. When you are indifferent, you cannot create a master mind alliance. A negative mental attitude will bring you nothing but failure.

"You must always remember that you are where you are and what you are because of your mental attitude and how you relate to other people. You must also remember that your mental attitude is the one and only thing over which you have complete control. Success is something that has to be planned. It is also something that must be earned in advance.

"Some say that people become successful through luck. I would say that is true if the definition of luck is something that you can create yourself if you know these principles and make them a part of your very being. Success in the higher brackets of achievement is only available if you take others along with you. The best definition of success that I know of is this: Success is the knowledge by which to get whatever you want from life without violating the rights of others and by helping others to acquire it. The key here, Stanley, Lisa, is *others*. When your focus is on others and helping others, you will be rewarded for your efforts. You will never work a day in your life because your life will be about your passion and your definite major purpose.

"Remember what our good friend Napoleon says: Whatever the mind can conceive and believe, the mind can achieve."

He sat back in the chair. He was done. He had finished what he came to do.

We all sat in silence for a few moments taking in all he had said to us. He leaned over and picked up the poster. He read each one of the principles out loud.

"The Principals of The Message

"1. Faith

"2. Personal Initiative

"3. Self-Discipline

"4. Go the Extra Mile

"5. Enthusiasm

"6. Overcoming Adversity

"7. Positive Mental Attitude

"8. Accurate Thinking

"9. Creative Vision

"10. Cosmic Habit Force."

Then he smiled big at Josh and said, "How about we add another one on there?"

Josh handed him the pen and he most craftfully wrote in the bonus principle: The Master Mind. He set the pen down on the table, and we all took a moment to admire the list. This was moment number eight that will always be etched in my memory.

He broke the silence. "Well now, this has been most invigorating hasn't it? I must be on my way now. I have stayed much longer than I expected. That happens when I am enjoying myself."

Charles stood up and picked up his cane and hat. We all stood with him, not saying anything. Josh walked up to him and hugged him. He let out a laugh and gave her a big hug back. He looked over to Rachael, and she came for a hug as well.

"Listen here, little one. I am expecting big things out of you."

He then gave her another big hug.

He opened the door and was about to walk out, and then he stopped.

"Oh, there is one more thing. When you make the movie, could you get someone good to play my part? I want someone who has some real acting chops, an Academy Award-winner. Someone like Louis Gossett Jr." He paused for a moment and said softly, "Yes, he will do nicely."

Then he put on his hat, tipped his head, and walked out the door.

Epilogue

Two years have passed since our last meeting with Charles Montgomery III. We like to call it the last supper.

I finished my book entitled *Just Believe*. I now believe I am living within my definite major purpose, and I am now under contract to write two more books. I have been asked on several occasions to share my story at conventions and schools. *Just Believe* has gone on to become a number-one seller and has broken all sales projections.

Lisa purchased the gym she was managing and formed a master mind alliance with Kyle Hawkins. They now have five gyms and are beginning to franchise.

Josh and Rachael continue to grow. Josh is the starting pitcher on her school's team and has aspirations of playing professionally. She has excelled by her own personal initiative and by going the extra mile.

Rachael is following her dad's footsteps by writing. She has written several children's books that deal with loss and finding the seed of equivalent benefit from adversity. Stanley's publisher is planning to publish her third book this fall.

Cooper is also living within his major purpose when he and Stanley take walks and he chases squirrels.

Trost Moving Pictures and the Narrative Television Network, along with their distributor, Destiny Image Films, joined forces to produce Stanley and Lisa's story, *The Lamp*. It was used successfully to raise over $2 million for charity in conjunction with the associates at Pre-Paid Legal through the Light of The Lamp charity screenings. You can find out more about those at www. LightOfTheLamp.com.

Academy Award-winner Louis Gossett Jr. was cast to play the part of Charles.

About Tracy Trost

Tracy J. Trost has been in television and marketing for over 20 years. He has achieved multi-millions in annual revenue using the principles of the gifts presented in this book. While still casting the vision, he's now actively pursuing his dream of making feature films at Trost Moving Pictures. *The Lamp* is the third film produced by TMP.

Jim Stovall is the president of the Emmy Award-winning Narrative Television Network. He is the author of the bestselling book, *The Ultimate Gift*, which is now a major motion picture starring James Garner and Abigail Breslin. He has authored 15 other books that have been translated into over 20 languages.

Recommended Books:

Restored - 11 Gifts for a Complete Life by Tracy J. Trost
A Christmas Snow by Jim Stovall
The Ultimate Gift by Jim Stovall
The Ultimate Life by Jim Stovall
The Ultimate Journey by Jim Stovall

In the right hands, This Book will Change Lives!

Most of the people who need this message will not be looking for this book. To change their lives, you need to put a copy of this book in their hands.

> *But others (seeds) fell into good ground, and brought forth fruit, some a hundred-fold, some sixty-fold, some thirty-fold* (Matthew 13:8).

Our ministry is constantly seeking methods to find the good ground, the people who need this anointed message to change their lives. Will you help us reach these people?

> *Remember this—a farmer who plants only a few seeds will get a small crop. But the one who plants generously will get a generous crop* (2 Corinthians 9:6).

EXTEND THIS MINISTRY BY SOWING
3 BOOKS, 5 BOOKS, 10 BOOKS, **OR MORE TODAY,**
AND BECOME A LIFE CHANGER!

Thank you,

Don Nori Sr., Founder
Destiny Image
Since 1982

9/24 KD